LIAN | ROCH

BAYOU HEAT 9 & 10

ALEXANDRA IVY

LAURA WRIGHT

LIAN | ROCH
Bayou Heat 9 & 10

First Edition
Published by Alexandra Ivy and Laura Wright
978-0-9899907-2-1

Copyright © 2014 by Alexandra Ivy and Laura Wright

Editor: Julia Ganis
Cover Art by Patricia Schmitt (Pickyme)
Interior Formatting by Author E.M.S.

Published in the United States of America

LEGEND OF THE PANTERA

To most people the Pantera, a mystical race of puma shifters who live in the depths of the Louisiana swamps, have become little more than a legend.

It was rumored that in the ancient past twin sisters, born of magic, had created a sacred land and claimed it as their own. From that land came creatures who were neither human or animal, but a mixture of the two.

They became faster and stronger than normal humans. Their senses were hyper-acute. And when surrounded by the magic of the Wildlands they were capable of shifting into pumas.

It was also whispered that they possessed other gifts. Telepathy, witchcraft, immortality and the ability to produce a musk that could enthrall mere mortals.

Mothers warned young girls never to roam alone near the swamps, convinced that they would be snatched by the Pantera, while young men were trained to avoid hunting anywhere near the protected Wildlands.

Not that the warnings were always successful.

What girl didn't dream of being seduced by a gorgeous, mysterious stranger? And what young man didn't want to try his skill against the most lethal predators?

As the years passed, however, the sightings of the Pantera became so rare that the rumors faded to myths.

Most believed the species had become extinct.

Sadly, they weren't entirely mistaken...

Contents

LIAN

ALEXANDRA IVY

CHAPTER 1

The streets of the small town of La Pierre, Louisiana were empty and the handful of houses locked up tight.

It could be because it was well past midnight with the faintest hint of an autumn chill in the air.

Or maybe it was the fact that the town was perched on the edge of the bayous where anything might crawl out and attack the unwary. Including a race of puma shifters known as Pantera who the humans had just learned weren't creatures of myth and legend.

Yeah, that might make the locals a little twitchy.

There was, however, one business in town that was still open to customers no matter how late or dangerous it might be.

The Cougar's Den was the local bar that doubled as a meeting place for the Pantera.

The two-story wooden building was built on tall stilts with a tin roof that was faded to a miserable shade of mustard. There were also shutters painted a dull green that could offer protection during hurricane season, and a rickety staircase that had nearly been the death of more than one human trying to make their way home after a long night of drinking.

Inside there was the mandatory bar with tall stools, a cramped dance floor and a couple of shabby pool tables at the back of the long, darkly paneled barroom.

There was even an old-fashioned jukebox that was currently blaring out Lynyrd Skynyrd to the dozen Pantera males lined up at the bar or playing pool.

Perched on one of the stools, Lian sipped his chilled water, looking every inch a badass Hunter.

It wasn't just the fact he was well over six foot, with broad shoulders and muscles that looked like they'd been carved from granite. Or the dark hair that had been pulled into a long braid that hung to his waist. Or even the jeans and faded Iron Maiden shirt.

It was the restless hunger in the whiskey-gold eyes and the barely leashed violence that buzzed in the air around him.

Of course, the Suit seated next to him didn't look much more civilized.

Michel might be a Diplomat, but there was no mistaking the fact that a lethal predator prowled behind those cunning green eyes. Oh, and if that wasn't scary enough, there was also the skull-shaved head, and broad body that was currently covered by a casual cotton shirt that was tucked into his black slacks.

At the moment, he was tossing back his favorite shot of whiskey as Lian filled him in on the latest happenings in the Wildlands.

Raphael, the leader of the Suits, had been careful not to share too much information when he sent out word to call his Diplomatic staff home. They'd discovered the hard way that not everyone could be trusted. Not even among the Pantera.

"Hiss is a traitor?" the Suit breathed in horror. "Fuck me."

Lian nodded. There were a lot of 'fuck mes' going around the Wildlands over the past few days.

Not only because Hiss had been actively working with their enemies, but because the Pantera had been attacked by the disciples of Shakpi who'd been determined to sacrifice Ashe's baby.

Oh, and the fact that they had the evil goddess—who was currently unconscious and trapped in a human body—locked in a secluded cabin in the middle of the Wildlands.

"Yeah, that's the general consensus."

Michel gave a shake of his head. "Why would he betray us?"

"He claims the elders were responsible for the death of his family. Only—"

Lian halted, glancing around the room to make sure there weren't any humans lurking in the dark corners.

"Only what?" Michel prompted.

He pitched his voice low enough that it wouldn't carry. Even if there weren't any humans close enough to overhear his words, and the jukebox continued to blare out Sweet Home Alabama, he simply assumed that the place had been bugged.

At least in the public rooms.

Paranoid? Maybe. But the past few weeks had taught him that they had enemies hiding everywhere.

Hiss was proof of that.

Damn him to hell.

"Only Sebastian's new mate, Reny, is his sister."

Shock widened Michel's eyes. "Hiss's sister?"

"Yep."

"I thought his entire family was dead."

"That's what we all thought."

"Shit. I need another round."

Michel motioned to the tall, golden-haired male who was lazily washing glasses. The Pantera spy who was currently acting as a bartender tossed the bottle in Michel's direction, obviously sensing the Suit needed more than one shot.

Lian reached for his water, lifting it toward his friend. "At least we have some good news."

"We do." Michel abruptly smiled. "The babe."

Despite the fact they were ass-deep in trouble, the birth of Raphael and Ashe's baby was something they could all celebrate. The first child born to the Pantera in over fifty years.

"She takes after her mother," Lian murmured. "A true beauty."

"To Soyala," the Suit announced, his voice

deep in tribute as he touched his glass to Lian's. "Our future."

"To Soyala."

They both took a drink before Michel was setting aside his glass and studying Lian with a somber expression.

"Did Raphael tell you why he was calling the Suits back to the Wildlands?"

"He wasn't comfortable sharing the fact that Shakpi is still alive over the phone," Lian pointed out in wry tones. "Plus, he wants to hear firsthand what's going on in the world. He's worried about the humans and their reactions to learning the Pantera aren't just a figment of their imagination."

"Yeah, he should be." Michel rubbed the back of his neck, his expression troubled. "The stories of rabid man-beasts who sneak out of the swamps to eat babies and rape women are all over the streets of New Orleans. Half the population wants to drop a nuke on the Wildlands to get rid of the dangerous mutants, and the other half wants to gather us up and put us in protective custody." Michel gave a dramatic shudder. "I don't know which one scares me the most."

"No shit," Lian agreed with an answering shudder. "It's going to get even worse when they discover two of them were killed when they tried to get ahold of Ashe's baby."

Michel scowled. "They attacked us."

"You're the supposed expert on humans, dude," Lian reminded his friend. "You know they won't care that we were only protecting ourselves."

"True." His hand curled into a fist on top of the bar, a sudden heat blasting from his body. "For now, we're terrifying monsters who've stepped straight out of their horror stories."

"Exactly. They don't need a reason to want us dead."

There was a brief silence as they considered the potential clusterfuck that waited for them, then Michel gave a shake of his head.

"Okay, I get that things are tense, but Raphael can't expect us to cower in the Wildlands forever?"

Lian shrugged. "I'm guessing it's temporary, but right now our leader is a little—"

"Ape-shit crazy?" Michel helpfully supplied.

Lian gave a sharp bark of laughter. Raphael was always aggressive. Now he was downright...well, ape-shit crazy was the perfect description.

"Yeah, that about sums it up," he wryly admitted. "I don't blame him. Not only is he a new father to a baby who carries the fate of the Pantera on her tiny shoulders, but we have a half-dozen Pantera traitors we have to deal with, and a powerful deity who might awaken any second and continue her evil plot to destroy us."

"Fair enough." Michel poured himself another shot of whiskey. "Has anyone come up with any bright ideas of how to kill the bitch?"

Lian swallowed a sigh.

No one wanted the bitch goddess dead

more than he did, but he wasn't happy with his current assignment.

He was supposed to be a Hunter, not a damned babysitter.

"The Geeks are studying the ancient scrolls," he muttered.

Michel arched a brow. "Isn't that a little old-school for them?"

"Desperate times, *mon ami*."

"You can say that shit again. Did they find anything that can help?"

"Not really, but they did locate a few scrolls that'd been stashed at the bottom of the original receptacle," he said. The receptacle was an ornately carved chest that had been discovered in the back of the caverns. It was believed that it had belonged to Opela. Most of the writings contained a history of the Pantera, along with the laws that still governed their people. "They hope the hidden texts will reveal how Opela stopped her insane sister the first time."

"Why do they only hope?" Michel demanded. "Can't they tell?"

Lian folded his arms on the bar, his muscles bulging beneath the T-shirt.

"They're written in an ancient script," he explained. "The Geeks haven't been able to translate them yet."

Michel rolled his eyes. Lian didn't blame his friend. Like their current streak of bad luck wasn't enough. Now the scrolls they needed had to be written in some weird chicken scratches?

"So we're fucked?"

"Maybe not." Lian once again lowered his voice. "Xavier asked me to fetch some scholar who specializes in obscure languages and bring him to the Wildlands."

Michel blinked, looking exactly like Lian had felt when Xavier had approached him.

Baffled. And dubious.

Extremely dubious.

"How would a human be able to translate the words of a Pantera goddess?"

"He was trying to explain the tedious methods of philogy—"

"Of what?"

"Some fancy way of saying someone who studies languages."

Michel grimaced. "Christ."

Lian nodded in agreement. There was nothing like a Geek to make you feel like an idiot.

"Exactly. It all sounded like blah, blah, blah after a while. Still, if this scholar can help then I'll track him down and bring him back."

Michel remained confused. "Why do you have to track him down? Can't Xavier just invite him to come to the Wildlands? It's not like we're flying under the radar anymore."

Wasn't that the truth? Lian suppressed the tiny frisson of unease. He was trying to ignore the looming human confrontation. Right now he had more pressing troubles to deal with. One disaster at a time, thank you very fucking much.

"Supposedly this researcher is some sort of

hermit who never leaves his home," he told his companion. "Xavier didn't even have a name beyond GoliardRetro."

"What kind of name is that?" Michel demanded.

"Some nerdy screen name thing," Lian said. In all honesty he wasn't interested in the language professor. His job was getting the man to the Wildlands as quickly as possible. The Geeks would take it from there. "Xavier managed to trace the computer to a general location in the northwest corner of the state. I'm going in to find him and convince him to join us here."

"And if he doesn't want to come?"

A smile of anticipation curled Lian's lips, the song on the jukebox appropriately changing to Eye of the Tiger.

Or in this case...puma.

"I can be very persuasive."

Michel narrowed his gaze, studying Lian with an oddly curious expression.

"Why you?" he abruptly asked.

Lian blinked. "Excuse me?"

Michel leaned an elbow on the bar, his steady gaze never wavering from Lian.

"Why did Raphael choose you to go get this scholar?" he pressed. Michel might look like a Hunter, but he was a perfect Suit. He had the insatiable curiosity of a trained spy. Every stone had to be turned over before he was satisfied. "There are Hunters in Bossier City."

Lian glanced toward the window, half expecting to see a member of his extended family standing at the edge of the bayou, waiting to walk him home.

"Because I told him if I had to spend another day in my house I was going to shove my head in a wood chipper," he admitted in rueful tones.

Michel gave a sudden laugh. "That bad?"

Bad? Lian rolled his eyes. He could barely breathe when he was forced to spend more than a few hours in his childhood home.

"I have an entire family of Nurturers who are constantly looking for someone to smother," he said, his expression one of disgust. No one loved their family more than he did, but yeesh. A full-grown male didn't like to feel as if he was still in the nursery. "I swear to the goddess, I can't step out of my private rooms without one of them trying to brush my hair or slap a band-aid on one of my boo-boos, or shove a cookie down my throat." He shook his head. "Yesterday I twisted my ankle during a training session with Parish and my mother threatened to tie me to my bed if I didn't spend the afternoon resting."

"Awww." Michel smiled with mocking amusement. "It's sweet."

"It's...humiliating," Lian muttered. "If I don't get away I'm going to lose my fucking mind." Rolling his shoulders, Lian slid off the stool. "Speaking of which, I need to get on the road."

Michel stood, his expression somber as he placed a hand on Lian's shoulder.

"Take care, *mon ami*. These are dangerous times for a Pantera to be on his own."

Lian nodded. "Always."

The pretty cottage situated several miles south of Shreveport was built well away from the dirt path and hidden behind a tall hedge. And if that wasn't enough to discourage unwanted visitors, there were a number of nasty traps hidden around the property.

After all, a young woman living on her own couldn't be too careful, Dr. Sage Parker had always assured herself. And if that made her seem antisocial, well…so be it.

She had her work.

Not only as a researcher, but she taught online classes for a local college.

It was all she needed.

At least, that's all she would admit to needing.

If she spent her nights lying awake, a restless need that she didn't entirely understand plaguing her body, she wasn't going to admit it.

Not even to herself.

Finishing her breakfast, Sage left the sun-filled kitchen to enter the main room of the cottage that her father had transformed into a library.

The walls were hidden behind floor-to-ceiling shelves that held her rare collection of leather-bound books. In the center of the room was a long, glass case that held fragile texts that needed constant temperature control. And in the far corner was a small desk nearly hidden beneath the crates of books that had arrived during the past week.

Sage halted to pull her pale, silvery blonde hair into a lopsided ponytail. As usual, she'd forgotten to comb it when she'd climbed out of the shower. Not that it mattered. There was no one to notice if her hair was tangled, or her delicate features that were dominated by large grey eyes were bare of makeup, or her tall, slender body was covered in a pair of yoga pants and faded Harvard University sweatshirt.

Her mother had complained that she had too much of her father in her.

He'd been a history professor who'd been little more than a shadowy figure to Sage. More often than not he was off on some archeological dig. And when he was home, he spent his days locked in the library instead of devoting any quality bonding time to his only child.

Her mother, on the other hand, had been a local midwife who'd dabbled in voodoo. She'd been determined to have her daughter follow in her footsteps, but Sage had adamantly refused.

Okay, maybe she had some weird...abilities.

But she'd rather be labeled an eccentric scholar, than a witch.

Especially now that both her parents were dead.

With her hair out of her face, Sage reached for the box of protective gloves she always used when handling her books only to drop them on the worn carpeting when the sound of a startled male cry echoed through the air.

An intruder.

Holy...crap.

Instinctively moving to grab the silver letter opener off her desk, Sage headed out of the library and into her parents' bedroom that she'd converted into a storage area for her overflow of books.

It didn't occur to her to call 911. It would take the cops a half hour to get to her place. If they even bothered to come. Her mother had placed a curse on the local chief of police when he'd cheated on his wife. He'd laughed at first, then he'd broken out in painful boils. He still held a grudge.

The putz.

Pushing open the door, she tentatively stepped into the room.

At first she could see nothing through the gloom.

She kept the curtains closed to guard her books against the sun. Now she had to strain to catch sight of the intruder who was struggling against the net that had fallen over him the minute he'd forced open the French doors and stepped into the room.

Her first thought was that she was glad the net had been magically enhanced by her mother to keep any intruder trapped until Sage released them.

Clearly the man was furious and ready to do some damage.

But as she snapped on the light to get a good look at her unwelcomed visitor she forgot how to breathe.

Oh...my.

His male beauty hit her like a punch to the gut.

The dark, perfectly chiseled features. The long black hair pulled into a tight braid. And the eyes that smoldered with golden fire in the shadows.

There was a raw sensuality that shimmered around him, calling to her most feminine needs.

Without warning the gnawing hunger that had only bothered her at night was suddenly flooding through her body, the strange sensations making her heart race and her palms sweat.

Good lord. She swallowed, feeling as if her skin was too tight for her body.

She'd been aroused before. She'd even had sex, although it'd been a colossal disappointment.

But nothing had prepared her for the blistering awareness that sizzled through her as a rich, intoxicating male musk seeped deep inside her.

"What the hell?" the man snarled, glaring at her in fury. "Get me out of here."

She felt a ridiculous stab of disappointment.

Why?

Did she think he was going to be struck

with the same tingling, breathless fascination?

Yeah. Fat chance.

Holding the letter opener in front of her, she took a hesitant step forward.

"It's very rude to trespass," she informed him.

His hands gripped the net, his large body tense with outrage.

"Maybe if you answered your damned door I wouldn't have had to trespass," he said between clenched teeth.

Sage frowned, belatedly recalling the pounding she'd heard when she was in the shower. She'd assumed that it was the wind banging one of her loose shutters.

Now she shrugged, not about to admit that she didn't recognize the knock because no one ever came to see her.

That was just...pathetic.

"I didn't answer because I don't want visitors."

"Fine." The golden eyes narrowed. "I'm not looking for you, anyway."

Oh. Another stab of disappointment.

"Then why are you here?"

"I'm looking for Dr. Parker."

She frowned in confusion. Did he mean her father? Surely not. He'd passed away ten years ago.

"Why?"

He gave the net a frustrated shake. "Get me the hell out of here."

She clutched the letter opener, trying to ignore her uncontrollable reaction to the stranger.

Not easy. He really was a magnificent specimen of manhood.

Tall, muscular, starkly beautiful...

She shivered, heat licking over her skin.

Why was it suddenly so hot?

"Not until you tell me what you want with Dr. Parker," she forced herself to demand.

A low growl rumbled in his throat. "Xavier sent me"

Sage made a sound of shock. "XavierTopGeek?"

The stranger's eyes widened, something that might have been amusement shimmering in the golden depths.

"Top Geek?" He gave a sharp laugh. "Oh hell, I'm going to have to share that sweet nugget with my fellow Hunters."

"I don't understand."

All humor was wiped from the intensely male face. "You don't need to," he snapped. "Let me out or you're not going to like the consequences."

Sage frowned, turning to study a nearby pile of books. Her mind didn't work properly when she was looking directly at the intruder.

"Hush, I'm thinking..." Her inner debate of whether or not to try and contact the man she'd been chatting with online for the past few years was brought to a sharp and painful end as arms wrapped around her and she was tossed onto the nearby bed. "Eek."

She slashed the letter opener toward her attacker only to have it knocked out of her hand as the man leaped on top of her, pressing her into the mattress.

"Not so fun being trapped, is it?" he rasped, his eyes darkening as she struggled beneath him. Heat abruptly sizzled between them as his body hardened. "Although I'm beginning to realize there are a few unexpected benefits."

A combination of fear, and anger, and potent arousal exploded through Sage.

"Get off me." She slammed her hands against his chest, panic thundering through her.

Regret softened his harsh expression as he gazed down at her, but he refused to budge.

"Where is Dr. Parker?" he demanded.

"Why?"

"I need to speak with him."

"About what?"

He hissed in frustration. "Do you always answer a question with another question?"

"No." Sage grimaced. Even being held hostage by a stranger she found it impossible to lie. "Okay, maybe I do. It's a habit."

"Look, I have no intention of hurting you, but this is important," he said, an unmistakable sincerity in his voice. "Can you just tell me how to find the scholar?"

Sage cleared her throat. If Xavier had sent the man, then he couldn't be looking for her father. And it was obvious she wasn't going to get rid of him until he'd spoken to 'Dr. Parker.'

"You already have."

CHAPTER 2

Sage watched shock tighten the man's expression, something in the back of his eyes making her stiffen in alarm.

What the hell?

She could have sworn...

The thought wasn't allowed to fully form as the stranger pushed himself off the bed, glaring at her in disbelief.

"Is that supposed to be a joke?"

Sage pushed herself to a seated position, her body still carrying the heat and scent of him.

"Why would I joke?"

He scowled, folding his arms over his chest. "You're the expert in ancient languages?"

"Yes."

"You're—" He halted, giving a shake of his head.

"I'm what?"

"Young."

"Not really. I'm thirty-two." She tilted her chin. This was a familiar argument. "And not to boast, but I had my doctorate by the age of twenty so I've had more time than most to concentrate on my own research. Plus, I've been an adjunct professor for the past ten years."

He glanced around the room that was nearly overrun with books.

"You live here alone?"

She absently rubbed her hands over her bare arms. His presence seemed to fill the entire room.

"I think it's your turn to answer some questions."

He pressed his lips together, impatience crackling around him. Then, with an obvious effort, he leashed his temper.

"Ask."

Her hands gripped the handmade quilt that covered the bed. "Who are you?"

"Lian."

"Just Lian?"

He shrugged. "Just Lian."

She narrowed her eyes. He might be gorgeous, but he was clearly a jackass.

"You're a friend of Xavier?"

"More of a relation."

Hmm. There was something in the way he said relation that made her think he wasn't talking traditional brother or cousin.

"What do you want from me?"

"Xavier has several scrolls he wants you to translate."

Okay. That didn't seem so...creepy. She was contacted several times a week by people who wanted her expertise in decoding ancient texts.

She was, without false modesty, the best in the business.

Still, most of her potential clients didn't send someone to break into her house.

"Why didn't he just ask me? I would have had him mail them to me."

"The scrolls are too fragile," he said. "They can't be moved."

Sage was prepared for the complication. Her work often dealt with fragile parchment.

"He could scan them or even take a picture and send me the images in an email."

Lian took a step forward, studying her with an alarming intensity.

"I thought scholars salivated over the opportunity to get their hands on rare artifacts?"

She lowered her gaze, well aware that her face revealed her every emotion.

One of many reasons she didn't play poker.

"I don't travel."

He heaved a harsh sigh. "Why not?"

"That's none of your business."

"Do you have a medical condition?"

She swallowed a humorless laugh, shoving herself off the bed. A medical condition would almost be preferable.

"You've wasted enough of my day," she informed her aggravating guest. "You can leave the same way you came."

She started to edge past his large body only

to be forced to a halt when he deliberately moved to block her path.

"What's your name?"

"You know my name," she snapped.

"Your first name."

Her gaze moved to the forgotten letter opener on the ground. Not as protection. If this man wanted to hurt her there was nothing she could do to stop him.

No. But she wouldn't mind stabbing the annoying creature in the leg.

His persistence was pissing her off.

"Sage," she at last admitted.

"Sage." Her name rolled off his tongue with a hint of a Cajun accent. A tiny shiver raced through her.

Nope, she wasn't ready for that level of intimacy.

"You can call me Dr. Parker."

His lips twitched. "Fine...Dr. Parker." His brief amusement faded. "This is important."

Excitement fluttered in the pit of her stomach.

He was close enough she could feel his heat wrap around her, the spicy musk clouding her mind with thoughts of smooth, bronzed skin beneath her tongue.

Good lord. She needed to get this man out of her house before her brain turned to complete mush.

"So is my research, plus I have papers to grade and—"

"This is life or death," he interrupted sharply.

"If you say so."

A strange growl rumbled in the air. Was that coming from Lian?

"Did you hear me?"

"We all believe our work is vital."

"No." He grabbed her chin, tilting back her head so she was forced to meet his fierce gaze. "This is a matter of life and death."

Heat blasted through her at his touch.

"Would you please…" Her words faltered as she once again caught sight of that shadow moving in the back of his eyes. There was something in there. Something that was focused on her with the smoldering hunger of a predator. "Oh…you're not human."

Lian cursed at his odd reaction to the female.

It wasn't just his astonishment at discovering that she was a she, not a he. Or even that she wasn't the old, slightly batty professor he'd been expecting.

It was the intense, blistering awareness that had slammed into him the second she'd stepped into the room.

Man. He could think of nothing but the overwhelming need to somehow get her beneath him so he could be buried deep inside her.

It was only because he'd been pissed as hell at being caught sneaking into the cottage—like he was nothing more than an unskilled cub—that had allowed him to leash the animal inside him that was roaring for a taste.

There would be no ravaging until he had her in the Wildlands, he'd warned himself.

Now he realized that his intense awareness had allowed him to overlook the obvious.

There was no way in hell he should have been trapped in that net unless there'd been a magical spell attached to it.

"I see your cat," she murmured, looking more curious than frightened.

Lian gave in to the impulse to run his fingers down her cheek, savoring the warm satin of her skin. This female obviously had magic running through her veins.

But it was the fact she could detect the animal inside him that made his heart leap.

Could she be a Shaman?

The mere potential was a cause for celebration.

There was an elder Shaman at the Wildlands who had long ago retired, and of course, Chayton, who was now lying unconscious with an evil goddess trapped inside him. Neither had been capable of serving his people for the past thirty years.

To have a young, clearly healthy Shaman just when the Pantera could once again breed would be nothing less than a miracle.

Suddenly the need to get her to the Wildlands became even more vital.

"How do you see my cat?" he asked.

"I just...do." She licked her lips, sending a jolt of white-hot excitement searing through Lian. Oh, hell. The things those lips could do to his body. "Is Xavier a cat as well?" she demanded.

He nodded. "Yes."

She wrinkled her brow. "I'm surprised I didn't suspect."

Lian scowled. He didn't know where the completely irrational stab of jealousy came from, but he sure as hell didn't like the implication she knew Xavier well enough to suspect he wasn't human.

Just how often had the two communicated?

"What do you know about my people?" he asked in abrupt tones.

"A great deal, actually." She glanced toward the stacks of books, offering Lian the opportunity to appreciate the delicate perfection of her profile. "I've read a number of books that describe the Wildlands and the puma shifters who live there."

"Do you know the legend of our creation?"

"There were two goddesses, Shakpi and Opela." She turned back to meet his watchful gaze. "I believe there was some sort of rift between the two."

His lips twisted.

Rift was a mild way of saying that Opela had sacrificed herself to lock her sister, Shakpi, in a prison so the crazy-ass bitch wouldn't destroy the Pantera.

"You could say that."

She tilted her head to the side, the end of her ponytail sliding over her shoulder.

Lian instinctively moved his hand to touch the silvery strands. Oh...man. It felt just like silk.

She stilled, but made no effort to pull away. "Are you a religious scholar?"

He gave a choked laugh. He fully admired the Geeks, but the thought of being stuck in a library or seated in front of a computer for endless hours gave him a brain cramp.

Give him open space, fresh air, and cunning prey to pursue and he was a happy cat.

Or give him a beautiful woman in his bed. Preferably one with silver-blonde hair and fascinating gray eyes rimmed with black.

"Hell to the no," he assured her, his fingers sliding around her neck to cup her nape. The crisp scent of lemon teased at his senses, the smell oddly erotic to the cat that stroked against the inside of his skin. It wanted a taste of this female. "I'm a Hunter."

"A Hunter?" She cleared her throat, pretending she wasn't burning up with an arousal that matched his own. A wasted effort. Her need was obvious in the flush that stained her cheeks and darkened her eyes. Even if he wasn't able to detect the sweet honey that was making her pussy slick and ready for his cock. "What does that mean?"

Maintaining his hold on her nape, he stroked his free hand down the curve of her spine.

"The obvious." He tugged her tight against his stirring arousal, his head lowering to press his face into the curve of her neck. "I track my prey until I have them cornered." He licked a rough path to the pulse that thundered at the base of her throat. "Then I pounce."

She made a strangled sound of shocked

pleasure, her hands grabbing his arms as if her knees had suddenly threatened to collapse.

"You're in my personal space."

He chuckled, rubbing his cheek against her smooth skin with a gesture that was pure feline.

"I'm deciding whether or not I intend to play with you before I pounce."

He heard her breath catch, her body instinctively arching closer to the hard thrust of his cock.

"I'm not your prey," she breathlessly protested.

Lian allowed his teeth to press into the flesh of her neck, not breaking the skin, but offering a warning.

He might be able to convince his cat to take the seduction of Dr. Sage Parker at a slower speed, but it wasn't going to tolerate any denial of the desire that smoldered between them.

"Of course you are," he growled. "I was sent to retrieve you."

She shivered, her fingers tightening on his arms even as she gave a shake of her head.

"I told you," she rasped. "I don't travel."

Muttering a curse, Lian lifted his head. As much as he wanted to toss this female on the bed and ease his throbbing cock deep inside her, he had to concentrate on fulfilling his duty.

They had to find some way to translate the newly discovered scrolls.

And for now, this woman was their only hope.

"And I told you. The future of the Pantera is depending on you," he said.

She pulled from his lingering touch, her hand pressed to her chest as if trying to slow the pounding of her heart.

"What makes the scrolls so important?"

He hesitated before giving a small shrug. She'd have to know the truth eventually.

"We hope it can tell us how to kill Shakpi."

CHAPTER 3

Sage felt the breath being wrenched from her lungs at the blunt explanation.

God almighty.

This was all happening too fast.

Her life was supposed to be a series of predictable, well-planned days that never varied.

She worked hard to make sure that there were no surprises.

Now her house had been invaded by a Pantera male. Her body was burning with an unfamiliar passion. She was being told she had to leave the safety of her house to travel to his homelands.

Then, to put icing on the crazy cake, he was implying that they needed her to translate a scroll that they hoped would kill a goddess...

Yeah. That tripped over the edge of what her poor brain could process.

"This isn't funny—" she started to sputter.

"Trust me, I don't joke about a psychotic goddess who's determined to commit genocide," he interrupted, his beautiful features grim.

Genocide?

She widened her eyes. "You suspect Shakpi is trying to destroy your people?"

"I don't suspect it," he snarled, the temperature of the room amping up a few degrees. Was the heat coming from Lian? "I know it."

"How?"

"She told us."

"Okay." She took a step backward. Until this moment she'd been willing to play along. But when people started saying they'd spoken directly to a god or goddess, and claimed to have direct knowledge of their holy plans, she had to draw a line. "And people think I'm crazy."

"I'm not crazy." He stepped forward, grasping her chin in his hand. "Listen to me, Sage. I'm going to give you the condensed version of Pantera history and then we're going to the Wildlands."

"I told you—"

"Just listen," he commanded, then, before she could remind him this was her house and she didn't take orders from anyone, he was swiftly revealing the events of the past months.

She wanted to laugh at his absurd story.

To assure him that he was out of his mind and that he needed to return to his home. Without her.

But the words wouldn't come.

Quite simply because she believed him.

Not only because of the sincerity in his voice, but because she'd always possessed the ability to sense when someone was telling her the truth.

She wasn't a lie detector. Her gift wasn't that precise. It was more an overall 'feeling' of honesty.

At last she gave a slow shake of her head and studied him with a growing sense of horror.

"You have a goddess locked in a shed in the Wildlands?" she breathed.

Lian turned to pace the worn floorboards, his movements possessing a fluid grace that no human male could match.

"Basically."

She wrapped her arms around her waist. "And you want me to translate a scroll in the hopes that it will reveal how to kill her?"

He turned, his face hard with determination. "Or return her to her prison. If she awakens and escapes she'll eventually discover a way to destroy us." He held her gaze, as if daring her to deny the truth of his words. "It's that simple."

She chewed the inside of her lip. She believed him. She didn't want to, but she did.

"You'll have to bring the scrolls to me," she at last conceded, holding up her hand as his lips parted in protest. "There are ways to ensure they're transported without harm and I'll need my research books to help with the translation."

"No."

Her brows snapped together. Annoying, arrogant...ass.

"You claim to need my help, then you go out of your way to be difficult," she protested. "It isn't logical."

He moved back to stand directly in front of her, his potent male musk making it difficult to think about anything but ripping off his clothes and exploring every inch of his hard, bronzed body.

"We can't allow the scrolls to leave the Wildlands when we're surrounded by enemies," he informed her.

She clenched her teeth.

Concentrate, Sage, she silently chided her embarrassing thoughts. The man was here to stop a potential genocide.

Now wasn't the time to be distracted by her suddenly overactive libido.

"What enemies?"

Fury flared through the whiskey-gold eyes. "The disciples of Shakpi have gone into retreat, but they continue to watch from the shadows for the chance to strike." He glanced toward the French doors, almost as if expecting to discover one of the disciples standing in the overgrown bushes. "If they learn that there was a scroll that could destroy their goddess they would stop at nothing to get their hands on it." His gaze snapped back to her, his expression bleak. "Including killing you."

Her heart squeezed in fear. Oh...lord. She spent her life trying to avoid attracting attention. The last thing she wanted was to piss off a bunch of homicidal fanatics.

"I can give you the name of another

translator," she said, inching toward the open door leading to the hallway.

If she was lucky, she could make a dash for her upstairs bedroom where there was a nice, sturdy lock on the door.

His eyes narrowed. "Are they as good as you?"

She shrugged, taking another step toward the door. "I know several who are very competent."

His lips twisted as he deliberately stepped into her path, his arms folded over his chest.

Busted.

"Who is the best?" he prodded.

She heaved a resigned sigh. "I...I can't come."

"Why not?" He reached to cup her cheek in his palm as she tried to turn her face from his unwavering scrutiny. "Dr. Parker?"

She forced herself to pull away, latching onto the first excuse that came to mind.

"I should think it was obvious," she said. "I am a genius, after all."

"What's that supposed to mean?"

"I'm smart enough not to take off with a stranger who broke into my home and claims he needs me to help kill a goddess."

"Good point." The cat lurked in his eyes...lethal, prepared to pounce. "Now tell me the real reason."

"I did." Her mouth was dry. Not from fear. No. This was pure, unadulterated excitement. "I think you should go."

He reached to trail his fingers down her

throat, hooking one finger into the neckline of her sweatshirt to pull her toward his hard body.

"You know I'm not leaving without you."

"Lian, don't."

He ignored her breathless protest, his gaze lowering to the full curve of her lips.

"Tell me, sweetheart. Why do you use these books to hide from the world?"

Trapped beneath the ruthless golden gaze, she found it impossible to lie.

"I'm different."

"Because you're smart?"

"That, and I..." She faltered. She didn't talk about her strange abilities. Not even with her mother, who'd always suspected her daughter wasn't normal. "I see things other people don't."

Most people would have laughed.

Or immediately assume she was a lunatic.

Lian didn't even flinch.

"What do you see?" He asked. "Images? People? His free hand reached to lazily play with the end of her ponytail. "Pink elephants?"

She glared at him. "It's not funny."

"I'm sorry." He went motionless, belatedly seeming to sense she was more than a little sensitive when it came to her 'gift.' "Please tell me," he urged in a soft voice.

A part of her wanted to walk away. This man already disturbed her on a level she didn't entirely understand. Did she really want to make herself more vulnerable by revealing her deepest secrets?

But another part sensed that this stranger

was one of the few in the entire world who could understand.

"When I truly looked at you I could see your cat. Not with my eyes, but..." She gave a shake of her head. "It's hard to explain."

His fingers cupped her chin, his attention focused on her with an unnerving intensity.

"What else?"

She blinked. His interest wasn't just a polite pretense. Or a fascination with the local weirdo.

It was a genuine, intense desire to know.

God. Could he actually reveal what was wrong with her?

"There are some people who have outlines of shapes that dance around them," she said, unable to actually describe the peculiar forms that she could see.

Some were so vague they were nothing more than wisps of white. Others were solid human outlines that were filled with vibrant colors. Yellow, scarlet, plum and a dozen other hues. Each color seemed to represent a characteristic of the form. Loyalty, honor, courage, anger, lust...

She wrinkled her nose. "I assume they're ghosts."

"Not ghosts," he corrected, his voice...reverent. "Ancestors."

Her heart gave a leap of hope. Yes. Ancestors who stood as protectors for their family.

That seemed right.

"How do you know?"

He gripped her hands, his eyes blazing with the force of his cat.

"Come with me, Dr. Parker," he commanded. "I have the answers you've been searching for."

The mansion in the Garden District of New Orleans was set behind high hedges and surrounded by a well-manicured lawn. The white two-story home was framed by a large pool on one side and a sunken rose garden on the other.

At the back was a large grotto that was surrounded by several marble statues that were rumored to have been stolen from Versailles.

The ten million dollar estate had once belonged to a prominent Louisiana family who were now buried beneath the recently remodeled garage.

Stepping onto the balcony that ran the full length of the second floor, Stanton Locke leaned against the ornate wrought iron balustrade and pressed his cellphone to his ear.

A tall man with dark hair he kept pulled into a short tail at his nape, he had a lean, dignified face, blue eyes and a slender form that was currently attired in an Armani suit.

The sort of man who looked as if he should be living in a posh mansion.

Few people would recognize him as the

brutally poor orphan who'd grown up in the East End of London.

Stanton, however, never forgot his cruel beginning. Or who had snatched him from the inevitable life of drugs and early death that had been his certain destiny.

"You managed to locate him?" He spoke into the phone, his British accent honed until it sounded as if he'd attended a posh boarding school.

"Yes," Hank answered him, his voice rough. Unlike Stanton, the local thug had no desire to try and better himself. Which was fine. There was always a need for expendable soldiers. "But it doesn't make any sense," Hank added.

"Explain."

"The house he's visiting belongs to some hermit researcher."

"Researcher of what?"

"Languages."

Stanton tapped an impatient finger on the railing, his mind racing.

Could this be the opportunity he'd been waiting for?

It was risky.

"A human?" he demanded.

"Yep."

"Intriguing." He paused, weighing the danger of tipping his hand against the knowledge they were running out of time. "We need that Pantera," he abruptly announced.

He heard his soldier suck in a shocked breath. "Are you fucking kidding me?"

Stanton understood the man's reaction.

Trying to capture a Pantera, even when they were away from their homeland, was like trying to trap a wild animal.

Thankfully they'd stumbled across the information that malachite could weaken the beast inside them, making it possible to bind them in the heavy-duty chains that Stanton had personally designed.

It wasn't always successful, as they'd discovered on more than one painful occasion.

But it was all they had.

For now.

"Ah, Hank, I did question whether you were suitable to take on a position of authority and clearly my fears were well-founded," he drawled.

Despite his lack of intelligence, Hank did possess a finely honed instinct for self-preservation.

"No..." he rasped, his fear throbbing in his voice. "I mean, of course I'll get him."

"Good." Stanton smiled, his gaze sliding toward the tree-lined street just visible over the high hedge. "You know what happens to people who disappoint me."

"Yes, sir. I'll contact you as soon as I have him."

"You do that."

Stanton returned the cellphone to his pocket, lingering on the balcony to enjoy the morning sunlight. The autumn air was crisp, but still warm enough to encourage him to delay his return to the house.

It was the unmistakable ping of his computer that at last forced him to turn and enter the long, ivory and gold room he'd chosen as his office.

The lofted ceiling with gilt cornices matched perfectly with the Louis XIV furniture and Persian carpets, creating a Versailles vibe. The ornate elegance might offend some men, but Stanton had spent his early days dreaming of the day he would be surrounded by luxury.

This suited him just fine.

Crossing to the cherrywood desk, Stanton settled himself in his chair before he touched the button on his computer to connect with the caller.

"Yes, master?"

The screen flickered, but it remained too dark to reveal more than a vague outline.

"Have you managed to retrieve my prize?" a dark voice demanded.

Stanton felt a chill inch down his spine. He'd only seen his master in the flesh on one memorable occasion. He still had nightmares.

But the man had turned Stanton's life from one of grim survival to endless possibility.

For that he was willing to give him unwavering, unconditional loyalty.

"We are still searching," he was forced to admit.

The man made a sound of annoyance. "My patience grows thin."

"I understand," Stanton soothed. "I have several warriors poised to infiltrate the Wildlands, but the Pantera remain on heightened alert." He resisted the urge to clench his hands in frustration. Emotions were the enemy. Success came from a clear head and a precisely formulated plan. And if events outside his control interfered in his scheme, then it was his duty to find a way to use that interference to his advantage. That was how he'd earned his current position on top of the Organization. And how he intended to stay there. "It is impossible to enter their territory unnoticed."

There was a husky rattle as the Master struggled to breathe. "What we need is a distraction."

"My thoughts precisely," Stanton promptly agreed. "I hope I might have one."

"The sooner the better, Stanton." The warning was unmistakable. "For all our sakes."

CHAPTER 4

Sage felt hope spike at Lian's soft promise to reveal the truth of her strange powers, only to be swiftly replaced by a wary disbelief.

"How could you know what's wrong with me?" she demanded, pulling her fingers out of his hands.

He scowled, but he allowed her to step away. "To start with, there's nothing wrong with you," he growled.

"I'm not normal."

"Thank god," he assured her. "Normal is boring. You're blessed."

Blessed? She shuddered when she remembered the neighborhood children who ran away when she started to talk to the misty figures that no one else could see. Or worse, when she had a vision of a disaster before it happened.

Ah yes, and then there was the time she'd accidentally set the classroom on fire.

After that little incident her mother had decided it was safer for her to be homeschooled and she'd retreated into her father's library.

Even then she'd been harassed by her mother, who'd been convinced her 'gifts' could somehow be used to increase the family income.

"That's easy to say when you're not..."

"Different?" he helpfully offered when she hesitated. "Trust me, sweetheart, I know all about being different."

Okay. That was true enough. Still, it wasn't the same.

"But at least you know what you are, and you were raised with people who are just like you."

A wicked smile touched his lips. "Oh, sweetheart, no one is like me."

She rolled her eyes, even as her heart gave a leap of excitement.

He was just so...gorgeous. And charming. And sexy.

Sexy enough to melt a reclusive spinster into a warm puddle of aching need.

"You know what I mean," she forced herself to accuse. "You didn't have to worry that someone was going to think you were weird or—"

Her words were cut off as Lian unexpectedly pressed a finger to her lips.

"Shh."

She watched in confusion as he moved with a blurring speed to press himself against the far wall, tilting his head to peer out the French doors.

Sage froze, speaking in a whisper. "Did you hear something?"

"An intruder outside the house." He gestured toward Sage, waiting until she hesitantly moved to join him. "Do you recognize him?"

She glanced out the glass door, a sharp fear clenching her stomach at the sight of the large man with a shaved head and multiple piercings. Wearing a black motorcycle jacket and heavy leather boots, he looked so much like the typical 'bad guy' she couldn't believe he was real.

"No." She gave a shake of her head. "I've never seen him before."

They watched as the stranger pulled a gun from beneath his coat, unaware he'd been spotted as he began to wrestle his way through the tangled overgrowth of her yard.

For once Sage was happy she didn't have interest in keeping a neatly tended lawn. It would take him at least a few minutes to reach the house.

"I'm sorry, sweetheart, but time just ran out," Lian said on a low growl.

Her brows lifted as he turned back to reveal his obstinate expression.

"What do you mean?"

"We have to go."

She bit her bottom lip. "Go where?"

She knew the answer before he ever said the words.

"The Wildlands."

"No." She gave a violent shake of her head. "No way."

He reached to grab her shoulders, his grip firm enough to warn he was barely resisting the urge to toss her over his shoulder and force her to leave with him.

"Do you want to stay and see if he's in the mood to shoot you?"

Panic skittered down her spine at the mere thought.

"You could get rid of him."

He held her gaze, allowing her to glimpse the predatory cat that lurked just below the surface.

"Yes, but I don't think you'd like my methods."

She glanced back toward the man creeping ever closer.

Shit. He was right. She didn't want to force Lian to kill the intruder.

But the mere thought of leaving the security of her home and traveling across the state with a man who stirred her most primitive needs sent a flutter of nerves through the pit of her stomach.

"I can't," she breathed.

His hands lifted to cup her face, thumbs brushing her cheeks with a tender caress.

"I promise I'll take care of you, sweetheart." The heat of his hands scalded her skin, his musk wrapping around her to offer a drugging sense of comfort. "Nothing's going to hurt you."

Did she really have a choice?

There was no way in hell she was going to

stand around and wait for the scary man dressed in leather to break into her home.

But that didn't mean she had to like it.

"You've already put me in danger," she accused, assuming the man had to have followed Lian to her house.

She hadn't had a problem with gun-toting strangers before.

"Trust me." He reached to grab her hand, tugging her until she was pressed against the solid strength of his chest. "Can you do that?"

"I don't know," she admitted with a stark honesty.

Without warning he swooped down to capture her lips in a kiss that jolted through her with blistering pleasure. Sage gasped, her mouth instinctively parting beneath the enticing demand of his tongue.

Good lord.

Who knew a mere kiss could feel like she was being struck by lightning?

She shivered, her fingers clutching his T-shirt as he spoke against her tingling lips.

"Come with me, sweetheart," he urged.

"Fine," she grudgingly agreed, allowing him to tug her out of the room and toward the side door in the kitchen. "But I don't like this."

Keeping her hand tightly clenched in his, Lian steered her toward a small opening he'd obviously cut into the hedge surrounding her house. Then, keeping in the shadows, he moved along the dirt path at a swift pace.

Sage remained silent, periodically glancing

over her shoulder to make sure they weren't being followed.

There was something distinctly unnerving in the thought that there was a very real possibility of being shot in the back.

But after running for over a mile, her thoughts altered their focus from flying bullets to the growing ache in her side.

She was a researcher, not a marathon runner.

About to inform her companion she couldn't jog all the way to the Wildlands, Sage was caught off guard when Lian tugged her around a thicket of trees where a car had been parked.

No. Not just a car.

This was a sleek work of art.

"What is it?" she breathed in awe.

Lian ran a hand over the streamlined roof, a strange smile curving his lips.

"A Lamborghini Gallardo."

Sage didn't know much about cars, but she sensed the white automobile with black accents was worth a rather large fortune.

"It's yours?"

The sinful smile widened as Lian opened the passenger door so she could slide onto the butter-soft leather seat.

"Actually it belongs to Jean-Baptiste," he explained as he took his place behind the steering wheel, revving the powerful motor to life. "He's going to shit when he finds out that I borrowed it."

Despite the fear that continued to pound through her, she couldn't help but laugh.

The man was impossible, but he was so boyishly charismatic that she couldn't be mad.

"Borrowing implies that there was mutual consent," she informed him.

He stomped on the gas. "It was an emergency," he countered, taking obvious pleasure in flying down the road at a speed that made her hair stand on end. "And it was just sitting in the garage, begging to be taken. How could I resist?"

She shook her head. She'd bet her rare Kish tablet that this man had never heard the word 'no' before.

"Are you an only child?" she abruptly demanded.

"Nope. I have three older sisters."

"That explains it."

He sent her a quick glance. "Explains what?"

"Your assumption you should always get your own way."

He chuckled, his attention thankfully returning to the road. "What about you? Are you an only child?"

She turned her head to study the scenery that passed them in a dizzying blur.

"Yes, but I wasn't spoiled."

"Why not?"

She hunched a shoulder, her stomach cramping at the unpleasant memories of her childhood.

"My father was rarely home and my mother

washed her hands of me when I refused to embrace my gifts," she confessed.

"What about your extended family?" He was forced to slow as they hit the interstate. The morning traffic wasn't heavy, but she was certain the last thing Lian wanted was to be stopped by a cop. "Your grandparents and aunts and uncles?"

"I never met them."

She sensed his astonishment. Not surprising. From what she'd learned of the Pantera, they were a tightly knit community that put an emphasis on the pack.

"Never?"

"My father emigrated from England and my mother's family disapproved of her choice to practice voodoo." Her hand reached to unconsciously grab his hard thigh as they darted off the interstate and hit a side road with a sudden burst of speed.

She understood he was trying to determine if they were being followed, but...yikes.

"You must have been lonely," he said, taking several more turns before they were back on the interstate.

It took a minute for her to catch her breath. "Yes."

"I can't even imagine," he mused. "I was smothered to the point of near insanity. I love my family, but a male needs his space."

Her lips twisted, hiding the envy that sliced through her heart.

How many nights had she dreamed that she was surrounded by a loud, loving family that actually cared whether she did her homework or ate her vegetables?

"Spoiled," she said beneath her breath.

Naturally he heard her. It seemed they actually did possess the acute senses of a puma.

"Don't worry, they'll be anxious to smother you as well."

Her head jerked around to meet his teasing glance. "Me?"

"Of course."

"Why would they care about me?"

"Because they're Nurturers and they're morally compelled to fuss over people."

She scowled, telling herself that he was being ridiculous.

And even if he wasn't, she didn't want complete strangers fussing over her.

Did she?

"I won't be there long enough for anyone to notice me," she protested.

A mysterious smile touched his lips. "We'll see."

Knowing it was pointless to argue with the stubborn man, Sage settled back in her seat and concentrated on the world that whizzed past her. Anything to keep herself from thinking of how far away she was from the safety of her tiny cottage.

She lost track of time as Lian concentrated on weaving through the increasing traffic, one eye on the rear view mirror to make sure they weren't being followed.

Then, just as they reached the outskirts of

Baton Rouge, she was jerked out of her inner thoughts as a black truck zoomed from a side ramp and slammed directly into their rear bumper.

"Lian," Sage cried in fear, certain they were about to die in a fiery crash.

Lian, however, expertly turned into the spin, somehow managing to avoid the other cars as he whipped them around and then headed for the nearest exit.

"Hang on, sweetheart."

Lian didn't have the same skills as Jean-Baptiste behind the wheel, but he did have a car with a finely tuned engine that could hit two hundred miles an hour, and the lightning quick reflexes of a cat.

Within a few miles he'd managed to shake the black truck and disappear among the suburbs of Baton Rouge.

Still, he remained on full alert.

There was no way in hell the intruder could have followed them from his researcher's house.

Which meant that the bad guy had enough cohorts to watch the roads for the very distinctive Lamborghini. Or he'd managed to tag the car with a tracking device.

Either way, Lian had to get off the streets.

Winding his way toward the older district

that lined the banks of the Mississippi River, he at last turned onto a dead-end street that had seen better days.

Beside him Sage sucked in a deep breath, clearly suffering from shock.

"Why are you slowing?" she demanded in husky tones.

"We need to lie low for a few hours."

She furrowed her brow, studying the dilapidated homes and air of aging decay that shrouded the entire neighborhood.

"Here?"

"Trust me."

She brushed back a silvery curl that had come loose from her ponytail, her hand unsteady.

"As if I have a choice."

Lian pulled into a narrow alleyway, regret stabbing through his heart.

When he'd gone to collect the mysterious Dr. Parker for Xavier, he hadn't considered that he might put the man in danger. And even when he'd discovered that the researcher was a fragile young woman who was terrified to be forced from her home, he'd still insisted that she leave.

He'd been confident that he could protect her. That nothing could get past him to hurt her.

Now he realized that his arrogance had very nearly gotten both of them killed.

Shit. If something happened to this female he would never forgive himself.

Not only was she vital to the future of his

people, but his cat was insisting that she belonged with him.

There was nothing more important in the world than keeping her safe.

Halting in front of a chain link fence that blocked the path, he reached beneath the seat to retrieve his gun. Then, rolling down the window, he used his acute sense of smell to ensure there was no one lurking in the shadows.

Once confident they were alone, he swiftly left the car to press his hand to the sensor hidden in a box on the brick wall that lined the alley.

Instantly the gate slid open.

The locks were rigged to sense the touch of a Pantera, which meant as soon as the gate closed behind them, nothing but another Pantera could open it again.

Returning to the car, he drove past the fence and through a garage door that lifted as they approached.

As the door slid down behind them, the lights flickered on to reveal a large, surprisingly well-maintained space that was attached to the two-story Colonial-style home next door.

Climbing out of the car, Sage glanced toward the steel storage cabinets that held the expected tools and auto parts expected in a garage, as well as several emergency firearms and ammo.

"What is this place?" she asked.

Joining her, Lian placed a hand on Sage's lower back and urged her toward the door connecting the garage to the main house.

"A safe house."

They walked down a short hall, then together they stepped into a large, airy kitchen that had been recently remodeled to include white cabinets, granite countertops, stainless steel appliances and a white and black tiled floor.

Sage blinked, seemingly astonished to discover the inside didn't match the dilapidated outside, but her attention was clearly more focused on what might be hidden just around the corner.

"Are we alone?"

"Yes." He pulled his cellphone from his pocket, needing to pass along word of their attack, as well as getting help as quickly as possible. "Raphael has called most of the Pantera back to the Wildlands."

She nodded, wrapping her arms around her waist as she glanced toward the windows.

"What if they find us?"

He moved forward, brushing the back of his fingers down her cheek. "They can't get through the locks."

"How do you know?"

His heart twisted. Man. He hated the fear that edged her voice.

And the knowledge that he was entirely responsible.

"They're specifically designed to react only to a Pantera's touch. There's no way in hell any human could get past them," he said, not bothering to share the fact that there were traitors among the Pantera. She was freaked out enough. "Besides, I made sure we weren't followed." Leaning down, he brushed his lips over her forehead. "If you need the bathroom there's one just through the dining room, next to the office."

She gave a jerky nod, wiping her hands on her sweatshirt before she forced herself to head out of the kitchen.

Lian resisted the urge to yank her in his arms and offer her comfort.

She was still trembling from their nerve-shredding trip to the safe house. She needed time to gather her composure before she would be ready to accept anything from the male she no doubt held to blame for her current situation.

Completing his phone call to Raphael, he searched through the kitchen for something to make for lunch.

It would be a few hours before the nearest completely trustworthy Pantera could reach them. Until then, he intended to do his best to prove to his companion that he wasn't going to let her down again.

He'd demanded her trust.

It was time he earned it.

Opening a can of soup, he poured it into a pan and set it on the stove, then he pulled out a loaf of bread from the freezer along with sliced cheese.

He'd just laid the buttered bread in the hot skillet when Sage returned to the kitchen, her face pale but her expression calm.

"Are you hungry?" he asked, keeping himself busy as she settled on a stool that was pulled up to the breakfast bar.

The urge to touch and hold her was nearly overwhelming, but he compelled himself to be patient.

Not his finest talent.

Hell, it didn't even make the top hundred.

"Yes," she admitted. Not that she had much choice when her stomach gave a loud growl.

"How about a grilled cheese, and tomato soup?"

"You cook?"

He sent her a startled glance, the agonizing pressure in his chest faintly easing. Her teasing might be forced, but it proved she hadn't completely decided to hate him.

"Only the basics," he warned, spooning the soup into bowls as he finished browning the sandwiches and slid them onto paper plates. They were far from perfect. One side was too dark and the other barely toasted. But he couldn't deny a strange surge of pure joy as he watched her sip the soup and take a large bite of the grilled cheese. Ignoring his own food, he leaned his elbows on the counter and studied her with blatant pleasure. "To be honest, I rarely get the chance. Now I'm starting to understand why it makes my mother so happy."

She glanced up in confusion. "You are?"

"I like taking care of you," he told her in soft tones.

Her gaze dropped, a blush touching her cheeks. "I'm not a child."

His lips twisted as the violent awareness he was desperately trying to keep leashed blasted through him.

"Believe me, Dr. Parker, I'm painfully aware you're all woman."

Her blush deepened, the pulse at the base of her neck fluttering.

Not fear.

Arousal.

She cleared her throat. "How long are we going to stay here?"

Unable to resist temptation, Lian reached out to touch his fingertips to that pulse, his cat purring at the blatant assurance she was far from indifferent to him.

"Until Raphael can send someone to escort us to the Wildlands." His fingers drifted down to the loose neckline of her sweatshirt. Her warm, citrus smell filled the kitchen, making him instantly hard. "I'm not going to risk trying to move you without backup."

She polished off her sandwich, trying to pretend her heart wasn't racing as his finger slipped beneath her sweatshirt to trace the line of her collarbone.

"Why do you think they followed us?"

That was the question, wasn't it? Their enemies had one purpose, and that was to return Shakpi fully to this world. So far they'd infiltrated the Wildlands, lured a handful of Pantera into becoming traitors, and tried to turn the humans against them. So attempting to predict their next move was enough to give any poor Hunter a headache.

He gave a frustrated shake of his head. "Maybe they hope to kidnap me to use as leverage in getting ahold of Shakpi. Or—"

"Or?" she prompted.

He hesitated before finishing his sentence. Sage was too intelligent not to reason out what was bothering him.

"It could be they've learned you hold the potential to translate the scrolls."

"What if I can't?" She bit her lip, the stunning gray eyes shadowed with fear.

Not for herself. But at the thought of failing his people.

With a smooth leap he was over the breakfast bar and pressing a finger to her lips.

"You will."

"You can't be sure," she protested. "My skill with languages isn't magic."

His thoughts fragmented as his finger traced the full temptation of her lips.

There were a thousand reasons his thundering need to claim this female was a bad idea.

A demented goddess who might wake at any moment. Enemies who were even now searching for them. Sage's potential position as Shaman.

Not to mention the fact that the female was still feeling vulnerable.

But nothing could convince his cat that she didn't belong in his arms...oh hell, who was he kidding?

It wasn't just his cat.

The man very much needed her stripped naked and spread beneath him.

"You're magic," he assured her, lowering his head to bury his face in the curve of her throat.

She lifted her hands to rest against his chest, but they didn't try to push him away.

"What are you doing?" she demanded.

He shuddered. The raw ferocity of his need was enough to scare him, let alone a poor female who couldn't possibly understand how quickly a Pantera could become addicted to one special partner.

"I'm sorry." He nipped at her tender flesh, his arms sliding around her to tug her off the chair and against his chest. "I know I keep pushing you, but my cat doesn't understand why it can't have a taste."

She trembled, her head tilting back to give him greater access.

"A taste of me?"

A roar of approval rumbled in his chest at the open invitation, his tongue tracing the delicate line of her throat before he indulged in another nip.

The delicious, lemony taste of her exploded on his tongue. His hunger spiked. Oh, man. He was going to *devour* her.

"Maybe more than just a taste," he warned, the image of her spread across the breakfast bar searing through his mind.

She grabbed his T-shirt, as if her knees were threatening to collapse.

"Lian," she breathed.

He nuzzled the sensitive spot just below her ear. "Tell me no and I'll stop."

"And if I don't say no?"

CHAPTER 5

Sage felt Lian stiffen, clearly shocked by her low words.

Hell, *she* was shocked.

She was the typical scholar.

Introverted, socially awkward, and embarrassingly timid when it came to flirting.

But somehow this man managed to bring out a side of her she didn't even know existed.

When she was with Lian she wanted to be the sort of bold, daring, sexually exciting woman who could drive a man crazy. It didn't make sense. Certainly not when they were virtually strangers.

But in this moment, she didn't care.

She'd been alone for so long.

Too long.

Now her entire body hummed with a desire that she refused to deny.

Lifting his head, Lian searched her upturned face with a wary expression. She sensed that he expected her to have a sudden panic attack.

Not surprising.

She'd never been particularly courageous. Nothing at all like the Pantera females who he no doubt usually chose as his lovers.

The thought only stiffened her spine.

He gently cupped her cheek in his palm, his thumb stroking her lower lip.

"You're stressed."

His senses were too acute for her to lie.

"True."

Regret scorched through his golden eyes. "And I'm taking advantage."

She frowned, rebelling at the realization he thought she was too weak to say 'no' to his seduction.

Dammit.

She might not be Xena warrior woman, but she wasn't spineless.

Fisting his shirt in her hands, she went on tiptoe to kiss him with a blatant need.

"I might not be a Pantera Hunter, but I'm not completely helpless," she warned, biting his lower lip hard enough to make him hiss with pleasure. "If I wanted to stop you, I would."

A sudden heat blasted from his body, his hesitation forgotten as his eyes glowed with a golden fire.

"Ah yes, I'd nearly forgotten your little trick of trapping me in that net." A slow, sinful smile touched his mouth as his arms tightened around her. "Someday you're going to pay for that."

The tension that had gripped her since being forced from her home was seared away as she arched into the hard warmth of his body.

"It isn't my only trick," she whispered, rewarded for her bashful flirtation when he gave a soft purr of appreciation and abruptly swept her off her feet.

"I have a few of my own," he promised, rubbing his cheek against the top of her head.

Sometimes he was such a cat.

"Where are we going?"

"I need to have you someplace more comfortable."

She wrapped her arms around his neck, vaguely aware of the glossy paneling and tiled floors as he headed toward the stairs at the back of the home. She'd already discovered when she went in search of the bathroom that the house was beautifully maintained, despite the appearance from the outside, with all the modern conveniences a person could want. Now she had far more important things to occupy her mind.

They entered the nearest bedroom that was decorated in a pale ivory and lilac. Without hesitation Lian was crossing the floor and lowering her onto the massive four-poster bed.

Sage's heart thundered in her chest, the spicy scent of his musk stirring her arousal until she could feel a damp heat bloom between her legs.

Straightening, Lian stared down at her, his entire body Hunter-still as he studied her with a predatory gaze.

She shivered, her mouth dry. Everything

about this man screamed danger, but she'd never been more excited in her life.

"You have me more comfortable," she husked, the anticipation flowing through her like the finest aphrodisiac. "Now what are you going to do to me?"

"First I'm going to strip off these highly unnecessary clothes."

Moving to plant one knee on the side of the mattress, Lian leaned down to grasp the hem of her sweatshirt, tugging it over her head with a smooth motion. He offered her a boyish grin of satisfaction as he easily performed the same service for the rest of her clothes, revealing that this was far from the first time he'd stripped a woman.

But once she was stretched naked on the lilac comforter his amusement faded, to be replaced with an expression of savage ferocity.

"Oh shit," he muttered.

She licked her lips, struggling to breathe. God. She needed to feel his hands on her skin.

It was becoming a near painful force.

"Is something wrong?"

"Hell no," he growled, his heated gaze inspecting her with unnerving intensity. "You're perfect."

"Aren't you going to take off your clothes?" she urged in husky tones.

As if sensing she wasn't as bold as she wanted him to believe, Lian swiftly stripped off his clothing, standing in front of her like a bronzed, exquisitely sculpted work of art.

Her eyes widened. God almighty. She'd never seen anything more beautiful. He was all male. A feral animal with his broad chest that tapered to a narrow waist and the long, muscular legs.

On his upper right shoulder she could glimpse a stylized tattoo of a crouching puma that looked ready to pounce.

And then there was the proud thrust of his arousal...

Her stomach clenched, her breath hissing between her teeth.

Okay. She needed this man.

Now.

"Better?" he murmured, watching as she stirred with restless frustration.

Daringly she patted the mattress. "You should be here."

"Soon," he assured her, placing a hand next to her head as he leaned over her. "First I intend to lick you from head to toe."

"That sounds—"

Her words were forgotten as his lips captured the hard point of her nipple.

She gasped as his tongue flicked over the tender tip, teasing her until she was arching in need. Good lord. She'd never felt anything so amazing.

It was as if she'd waited her entire life for his touch.

Licking and biting his way to her other breast, he reached up to tug her hair out of the rubber band to allow it to tumble over her shoulders.

Instantly his fingers smoothed through the silvery strands.

"Such glorious hair," he sighed. "Like liquid moonlight."

"Can I feel yours?"

The gold of his eyes darkened, his cat lurking just beneath the surface.

"God, yes," he pleaded.

He held perfectly still as she slowly undid the long braid, delighting in the midnight texture.

"It's soft," she said in a wondering tone. "And it smells like musk."

She combed her fingers through the long strands, allowing it to brush over her naked skin. The sensation triggered a low groan of approval from her parted lips.

"You smell like summer. Warm days and lemonade," he breathed, his hands tracing a scorching path over her body even as his teeth sank into the base of her throat.

The feel of his bite should have shocked her.

Instead she squeezed her eyes shut as her back arched with excitement.

"Lian," she cried out.

"I told you I was going to taste you." He returned his attention to her breast, tormenting the tip with his tongue as his hand eased between her legs. "Slowly." One finger slid between her slick folds. "Thoroughly."

"Does it have to be slow?" she rasped as he pressed his thumb against her clit.

"Oh sweetheart, we can go any speed you want later." He used the edge of his teeth to bite her nipple before he soothed the small pain with nuzzling kisses. "But this first time I want to savor."

Her hips instinctively lifted off the mattress as his finger slid into her aching body, his thumb rubbing her sensitive bundle of nerves at a steady pace.

"Savoring is good," she decided, her voice thick with need.

He gave a soft chuckle. "Just good?"

She tentatively slid her hand down his back, fascinated by the heated silk of his skin. She hadn't expected fur. Not in his human form. But who knew that he would be so smooth? And hard. And delectable.

"Maybe excellent," she conceded.

"Maybe?" Nuzzling a path up her neck, he teased the corner of her mouth before he kissed her, a stark demand. Sage melted, allowing her tongue to tangle with his as his finger thrust deep inside her. "I see you're one of those tough professors," he at last whispered against her lips. "What does it take to get an A from you?"

Sage scraped her nails over the rippling muscles of his back, delighted when he shuddered in pleasure.

She could have told him that the few classes that she taught online had earned her the nickname 'Hard-Ass Parker.' Right now, however, she was fully prepared to be generous.

Especially as he kissed a path down to her aching breasts, giving each nipple a lingering caress before heading ever lower.

"Sometimes I grade on the curve," she assured him.

He glanced up, his eyes smoldering with a hunger that sent a thrill of anticipation inching down her spine.

"A challenge," he said, his expression one of wicked promise.

Sage tried to swallow, her body vibrating with an acute tension.

"Not really—" Her words broke off in a strangled cry as his lips skimmed down the flat plane of her stomach. Her fingers clenched in his hair, her muscles trembling with delicious anticipation. "Oh."

He traced the curve of her hip, the abrasive sensation of his five o'clock shadow against her skin oddly erotic.

"I thought some extra credit would help."

"It's—" She hissed as settled between her legs and licked the liquid heat that pooled in her pussy.

Raw lust blasted through her, making her toes curl and her thoughts fracture.

"Yes?" he teased, tugging her legs farther apart.

"Stop talking," she commanded, sliding her foot down his bare back.

His eyes sparkled with mischievous humor. "Yes, Dr. Parker. I was always better with my hands." Another mind-destroying lick. "And tongue."

Oh, yeah. He was really, really good with his tongue, she silently applauded.

Running her foot up and down his back, she

groaned in pleasure as he fucked her with his finger at the same time he licked her clit with skillful expertise.

She writhed beneath him, desire spiraling toward a critical peak.

"Lian," she hissed in warning.

Easily sensing she was close, Lian kissed his way back up her body, balancing on his elbows as he peered down at her.

"I see your cat," she murmured, hypnotized by the feral wildness that lurked deep in his eyes.

"And he sees you." His voice was rough as his animal prowled near the surface. "He wants you in the worst way. Are you ready?"

She groaned, her hands cupping his face as she allowed him to see the depth of her need.

"So ready," she rasped, not about to confess that after years of celibacy she'd been ready for him the instant he'd snuck into her cottage.

That was just...pathetic.

"Thank god. I don't think I can wait another second," he confessed, his musk teasing at her senses. "You've gutted me, Dr. Parker."

Her fingers explored the chiseled line of his jaw before moving down to chart the broad width of his shoulders.

"Is that bad?"

He pressed a kiss to her forehead. "We're both about to find out."

Even prepared, Sage cried out as he angled his hips and pierced her with one smooth thrust. Good lord. She felt invaded.

Stretched to the limit, until she slowly became accustomed to his large cock.

She grasped his shoulders, shivering as his hair slid around them like a curtain of satin as he rocked in and out of her, each time thrusting deeper.

It was slow and tender and shockingly intimate.

She was being overwhelmed by Lian, lost in the heat and beauty of the moment.

The thought should have terrified her. She was a reclusive spinster who never allowed anyone close. But at this moment she wanted—no, she *needed*—to share herself on a primitive level.

Muttering low words of encouragement as she lifted her hips to meet his growingly urgent thrusts, Lian cupped her breasts, using his thumbs to tease at her nipples.

Sage groaned, digging her nails into his shoulders as he hit a magical spot that made her gasp as shocking pleasure jolted through her.

"Lian."

"I've got you, sweetheart," he muttered against her mouth, his body pressing even deeper.

She struggled to breathe.

She was close.

So deliciously close.

His hands lowered to grasp her legs, urging them around his hips as he pounded into her. At the same time, he buried his face in the curve of her neck, sinking his teeth into the tender flesh.

She screamed as her orgasm slammed into her with shattering force at the same time Lian groaned and released his seed deep inside her.

Bliss splintered through her before she was slowly floating back to earth, wrapping her arms around Lian.

She held him close, wishing this moment never had to end.

For the first time in forever, she wasn't alone.

Lian reluctantly pulled out of Sage's body, pressing his lips to the mark he'd made on her neck before he was gently gathering her boneless body into his arms.

Gutted indeed, he wryly conceded.

It wasn't just the savage ferocity of their lovemaking.

That had been...spectacularly fantastic. And he fully intended to indulge his sexual hunger as frequently as Sage was willing.

But it was the soul-deep realization that destiny had just crashed down on him that made him smile in wonderment.

His mate.

His cat had known from the minute he'd caught her citrusy scent, although his human nature had taken just a little longer.

It was, after all, a life-changing event.

Now both sides were in perfect agreement.

This woman belonged to him.

And he was never going to let her go.

Silently running his fingers through the silken strands of her hair, he contemplated how long he had to wait before informing her that she was fated to spend the rest of her life with him, when the chime of his phone made him groan in frustration.

Reluctantly releasing his hold on Sage, Lian rolled off the mattress and dug his phone out of the pocket of his jeans.

"Damn," he muttered, reading the text message.

Sitting up, Sage modestly tugged the sheet up to her chin. As if he hadn't kissed every satin inch of her pale skin.

"What's wrong?" she asked.

"Our escorts are almost here."

A satisfying hint of disappointment darkened her eyes to charcoal.

"So soon?"

"They were coming from Bossier City," he said, not sharing the information that they'd been traveling through the south to gather families of the Pantera and return them to the Wildlands.

He'd already terrified her enough, thank you very fucking much.

"Oh."

Lian watched in amusement as she scrambled off the bed and hastily began to jerk on her clothes.

Clearly she was embarrassed by the thought of getting caught in bed during the middle of the day.

He dressed at a much more leisurely pace,

anticipating the pleasure of challenging that modesty on a regular basis.

Not that he would ever change her.

His shy, scholarly beauty was perfect.

But Pantera were openly affectionate creatures who craved touch from their mates. And of course, his family was extremely high maintenance when it came to demanding attention.

It was going to be interesting to watch her adapt.

Crossing the short space, he smoothed her hair behind her ears and dropped a kiss on her forehead.

"It's okay. They're going to wait for us in the garage," he assured her, a stab of fear twisting his heart as he felt her stiffen beneath his touch. Lifting his head, he studied her with a growing concern. "Hey, are you okay?"

Her lashes lowered to hide her expressive eyes. "Why wouldn't I be?"

Blatant deflection.

His thumbs brushed the inside of her wrists, monitoring the unsteady pulse.

"Because we both know things just changed between us," he said, unwilling to try to pretend their time together was anything less than life-altering.

She kept her head lowered. "I don't know what you're talking about."

He clicked his tongue, releasing her hands so he could gently tip her face up to meet his wry smile.

"For the record, you're a piss-poor liar."

She heaved a small sigh. "I need time to...process."

He wrinkled his nose, sliding a finger down the length of her jaw.

"I'm pushing again."

"Yes."

"Sorry."

She arched a brow, her lips twitching with a burst of humor.

"No, you aren't."

Relief jolted through him. She might be stunned by the force of their attraction, but she wasn't frightened.

At least not yet.

"Busted," he admitted with a chuckle, rubbing their noses together. "It's my nature to go for the kill, but anytime you need me to back down just tell me, sweetheart." He stole a soft, lingering kiss. "I don't ever want you to feel overwhelmed."

"Hmm." She gave a tug on his hair. "I suspect you overwhelm most people."

True. He didn't have the brooding intensity of a Raphael or Parish, but his feral power tended to make most people avoid pissing him off.

"Not you," he swore, holding her gaze. "Never you."

Unexpectedly she reached up to thread her fingers through his hair that he hadn't bothered to braid.

Hell, he might never braid it again if Sage liked it loose.

And if that made him pussy-whipped...good.

"Only in the best way," she assured him in husky tones.

On cue his entire body went up in flames, his erection pressing painfully against his zipper.

"Oh hell, Dr. Parker, you might be a genius, but your timing sucks," he growled, wrapping his arms around her so he could press her tight against his aching cock. Then, knowing it was going to leave his balls blue, he kissed her with an urgency that had both of them panting before he reluctantly released his tight hold and headed toward the door. "Wait here," he muttered.

Promising himself an entire month alone with Sage once the scrolls were translated and the threat from Shakpi ended, Lian made his way through the safe house into the attached garage.

He caught the scent of the waiting Hunters before he ever pushed open the door. Which meant he was prepared to discover Mercier standing in the center of the cement floor. The dark, sable-eyed male had a broad, heavily muscular body that was currently covered by a white tee and camo pants. It took a second, however, to locate the other Hunter who was hidden beneath Jean-Baptiste's Lamborghini.

"Any problems?" he asked Mercier, ignoring the older male's narrow-eyed gaze.

There was no disguising the scent of sex that clung to his body, but he wasn't prepared to discuss his bonding with Sage. Not until she'd accepted that she belonged to him.

With a shrug, Mercier conceded to the unspoken warning.

"Nothing obvious, but..." The male scowled, giving a shake of his head. "Something's out there."

Lian knew exactly what he was talking about. It wasn't a precise smell, or a tangible sound. Just a vague sense they were being watched.

"Yeah, I'm getting the same vibe," he muttered.

Dammit. He wasn't afraid of his enemies. But how the hell did you fight them when they lurked in the shadows?

There was a muffled growl before Rosalie was sliding from beneath the car, holding her hand up.

"I found it," the tall, golden-haired beauty proclaimed, her pure green eyes smoldering with grim satisfaction.

The two males moved to inspect the tiny tracking device that'd been hidden on the undercarriage.

"Shit," Lian muttered, wondering if it'd been attached to the car while he was at The Cougar's Den or if it had happened while he was in Sage's cottage. Either way, he now knew how they'd followed him. "That didn't come from Radio Shack."

"No." Mercier's expression was hard as he plucked the device from Rosalie's fingers to inspect it with an expert eye. He was one of the Hunters who worked closely with the Geeks to develop weapons to protect themselves in the event the magic surrounding the Wildlands ever failed. "Military grade."

"Our enemies seem to have stepped up their game," Rosalie said, her puzzled expression reflecting her companion's growing confusion.

The disciples of Shakpi had always shown a preference for low tech, using the mystic power of their evil goddess to destroy the Pantera.

When had they gained access to this sort of equipment?

Lian made a sound of annoyance. "What the hell are they up to?"

"I don't intend to find out," Mercier snapped, taking charge. "Rosalie and I will drive your car along with the tracker and head west. Wait an hour, then go south with your cargo," he commanded. "We'll meet you back at the Wildlands."

Lian resisted the urge to argue. As much as he hated putting anyone else in danger, he had to concentrate on making sure that Sage was safe.

Besides, there were few things the two Hunters couldn't handle.

"Don't take any unnecessary risks," he ordered.

"*Moi*?" Mercier widened his eyes with a faux innocence. "Would I do that?"

"Don't worry," Rosalie said before Lian could remind his fellow Hunter of the day he'd leaped in front of a human poacher who'd been about to shoot a red fox who was nursing her young. Mercier had taken the shot to his chest, but had never halted as he grabbed the gun from the human and broke it in two. "He does anything stupid and I'll put his balls in a vise."

Mercier sent his a companion a heated glance. "I have a better place for my balls."

Rosalie leaned forward to nip the male's chin with an astonishingly intimate gesture.

"Keep it up and you won't have any," she warned in a throaty voice.

"Ouch," Mercier breathed, looking as shell-shocked as Lian felt.

Holy hell.

He hadn't seen that coming.

"Just be careful," he said, not surprised that neither noticed when he walked out of the garage and headed back to his waiting mate.

CHAPTER 6

The morning sunlight streamed through the open windows as Sage made her way down the narrow staircase of the large three-story house.

It'd only been two days since she'd arrived at the Wildlands, but she'd already been overwhelmingly welcomed into Lian's family, even as he'd been condemned to reside at the communal home of unmated Hunters.

She smiled at the sound of half a dozen voices all speaking at once that greeted her before she ever stepped into the large kitchen.

She'd lived alone for so long the noise and constant chaos that filled the Pantera home should have been overwhelming. And, at times, she couldn't deny it did make her head spin. But overall, she savored the warmth and companionship that surrounded her.

Sensing her arrival, the crowd of people that included Lian's grandparents, his parents, his eldest sister and her mate, all turned to regard her with blatant interest.

"Here she is," the silver-haired grandmother said, wiping her hands on a flower-patterned apron.

Lian's father moved forward to press a cup into her hand, his lean face that reminded her strongly of his son wreathed with a kind smile.

"Your coffee, just as you like it."

She wrapped her hands around the cup, a dangerous stab of pleasure warming her heart.

No one had ever known how she took her coffee.

Not ever.

"Thank you." She sipped the hot liquid. "It's perfect."

Lian's mother wasn't about to be outdone as she handed Sage a large bagel that was fresh from the oven.

"And a warm bagel to tide you over until breakfast," she said.

Lian's sister had the same dark hair and eyes as her brother although her face was far more rounded, with pretty features. Currently she was standing at the stove, frying bacon.

"Yes, we had to hold back the meal until Lian could get here," she informed Sage.

Sage's brief sense of cozy comfort was shattered.

Being surrounded by his family had offered her an unexpected comfort, but spending time with Lian was just the opposite.

The minute he walked into one of the shabbily comfortable rooms her entire body prickled with a fierce awareness that was downright embarrassing. For god's sake, everyone in the house could catch the scent of her arousal.

It was humiliating.

And worse, she was beginning to feel as if something vital was missing when he wasn't nearby.

How could he have become such an important part of her life in just a few days?

It was obvious she needed to limit the time they spent in each other's company.

"Oh, he's coming for breakfast?" she asked in what she hoped was a casual tone.

Lian's mother sent her a teasing grin. "After being on duty during dinner last night you didn't think he would miss the opportunity to see you first thing this morning?"

"That boy can't keep himself away," Lian's father agreed.

"Like you could?" The silver-haired grandmother gave a roll of her eyes. "I remember having to lock the windows at night to keep you out of the house."

With an unrepentant grin the male moved to wrap his arm around his mate's shoulders.

"How could I resist?" He pressed a kiss to her dark hair. "She's still the prettiest girl in the Wildlands."

Lian's mother tilted her head back, regarding her mate with an open devotion that made Sage's heart ache.

"Flattery will get you whatever you want, my love."

Sage backed toward the door. "You know, I think I should be working on those scrolls."

"But what about breakfast?" Lian's sister demanded.

She took another step back. And another. "This bagel is really enough, thank you."

"Lian is going to be disappointed," his mother sighed.

"Nonsense. He's a cat. He likes the chase," his father announced, sending a Sage a nod of approval. "Smart girl."

Sage gave a choked cough, her entire body sizzling at the thought of being chased by the dangerous puma.

"Yes...well, I'll see you later."

Turning on her heel, Sage bolted from the house, swiftly making her way to the communal center.

The first day she'd been amazed by just how civilized the Wildlands truly was.

The few books that had mentioned the Pantera implied that they were savages who lived like animals in the bayous.

Nothing could be further from the truth.

There might be a large part of the secluded lands that remained gloriously untamed, but the Pantera lived in beautiful homes that were cleverly built to incorporate the thick cypress trees, and were draped with Spanish moss. There was also a communal area where the land had been cleared to create a manicured park where they shared meals or enjoyed lazy games.

Perhaps most shockingly, there was a modern medical facility, a guest house, and a mansion straight out of "Gone With the Wind" that served as the headquarters for the Diplomats as well as the computer whizzes known as Geeks.

She'd been amazed when she'd entered the large plantation-style structure with fluted columns to discover it was filled with high-tech computers and monitoring equipment.

Thankfully, she'd been shown to the top floor that held the Pantera's most fragile books and scrolls. She wasn't a complete idiot when it came to technology, but she preferred to feel the weight and texture of a book. To smell the leather and dust and crumbling paper.

It was like holding history in her hands.

As she entered this morning, however, she was careful to spread the five ancient scrolls across the long table that Xavier had shoved to the middle of the wooden floor.

Not only was the fraying linen too fragile to be handled more than necessary, but she'd at last realized that the scrolls weren't individual texts, but instead, they were each a part of a whole.

Now a sense of...rightness...flowed through her as she studied the lines of glyphs.

It wasn't just her years of research, or even a natural intelligence that allowed her to decipher complex symbols.

She possessed an instinctive gift that went way beyond most scholars.

Yet another secret she kept hidden.

Losing track of time, she was bent over the scrolls when a low, male voice whispered directly in her ear, shattering her concentration.

"Any luck?"

Straightening, she turned to discover Lian standing mere inches away. Instantly her heart lodged in her throat and a vicious hunger twisted her gut.

Even after three days in the company of the large, outrageously gorgeous man, the sight of him was still a punch to her gut.

It wasn't just the perfect, bronzed features, or the whiskey-gold eyes that smoldered with wicked charm, or even the chiseled body she seriously wanted to lick from head to toe.

It was the sheer...maleness that stirred her on a primitive level.

She wanted to crawl into his arms and never leave.

And the knowledge scared the hell out of her.

Not because she thought he would ever hurt her. She understood the dark possessiveness that he felt for her would ensure he'd always protect her, even from himself.

But her past had taught her that she was asking for pain to open herself to another.

People left. They always left.

And then she was alone.

Far better to keep her heart well-guarded.

And of course, there was that embarrassing problem of wanting to climb on top of him the minute she caught sight of him.

It took only a glance, however, to realize that Lian had reached the end of his patience.

"You startled me," she muttered, absently

pulling off the gloves she always used when dealing with fragile texts.

"Sorry." He crowded her against the edge of the table, his finger reaching to smooth a stray curl behind her ear. "I did knock."

She sucked in a deep breath, savoring the spicy musk that sent heat jolting through her body.

Good lord. If he could bottle that scent and sell it as an aphrodisiac he could make a bazillion dollars.

She cleared her throat. "I tend to become lost in my research."

His lips twitched, his fingers stroking a decadent line of fire down her throat.

"Lost or hidden?"

She stiffened. Did he know she was deliberately trying to keep a distance between them?

"I don't know what you're talking about," she tried to hedge.

His fingers circled her neck, blatant ownership in his light grasp.

"I warned you that you're a terrible liar, Dr. Parker." He brushed his lips over her forehead. "Not that I blame you. My family can be—"

"Terrifying?" She cowardly latched onto his unintentional excuse for her elusive behavior.

"That's one way of putting it," he said wryly.

She felt an instant pang of guilt. "They're very kind," she forced herself to admit. It was the truth, after all. "And they've made me feel very welcome."

His lips skimmed down the narrow length of

her nose. "Yes, they adore you, but they tend to overwhelm the unwary."

She shivered, her hands clenching against the temptation to run her fingers through the long, glossy strands of his dark hair.

Why did he leave it free to flow down his back? It was a constant temptation.

"Is there something you needed?"

"Just to be near you," he said with his usual blunt honesty. Then he held up a hand that held a wicker basket. "And to bring you this."

Suddenly Sage's stomach growled as she was hit by the most delicious aromas.

Spice, and shrimp, and vegetables combined with a heady scent of freshly baked bread.

"It smells divine."

"My mother's gumbo and corn pone, still warm from the oven," he revealed. "She was concerned that you didn't eat enough breakfast."

"I wanted to get back to work," she said, turning to point at the scrolls she'd unrolled and aligned side by side. "During the night I realized that I'd been looking at the hieroglyphs all wrong. You see, it doesn't read from top to bottom, but across each scroll."

"Fascinating," he murmured.

She glanced up to discover him studying her with an unwavering focus.

"You're not even looking."

"Of course I am." Hunger shimmered in his eyes as they lowered to her lips. The air prickled with a heated arousal as he grabbed her hand and led her across the floor and through the French doors. "I just happen to be interested in something other than musty scrolls."

"Lian, I'm supposed to be translating," she protested even as she crossed the balcony and allowed herself to be seated at the small wrought iron table.

He efficiently emptied the wicker basket, taking the lids off the bowls of steaming gumbo and divvying up the corn pone. Then, pouring them each a glass of wine, he settled in the chair next to her.

"I admire your dedication, Dr. Parker," he said, taking a sip of the wine, the gentle breeze tugging at his hair. Even in the afternoon sunlight he looked dark and dangerous and entirely edible. "And I swear I'll do my best to give you all the freedom you need to pursue your interests so long as you give me permission to distract you when I think you need a break."

Anticipation licked through her body. "What sort of distraction?"

A slow, sinful smile curved his lips as he easily caught the scent of her arousal.

"First, we eat."

Sage sucked in a deep breath, grabbing for her spoon.

Yeah. Eat.

No jumping on top of the yummy Pantera and having her wicked way with him...

Concentrating on the food, Sage cleared her plate, giving a small groan at the savory burst of flavors. After years of surviving on salads and frozen dinners she could pop in the microwave it was a delight to indulge her senses with homemade meals.

Watching her lick her fingers with obvious satisfaction, Lian lounged back in his chair.

A big, lazy cat with the eyes of a lethal predator.

"More wine?" he asked.

"No." With an abrupt motion she was on her feet. She wanted to rub her cheek over his unshaven jaw so badly it was a physical pain. "I'll fall asleep."

With a fluid motion he was standing next to her, threading their fingers together.

"I know how to wake you up."

Instead of heading back inside, he pulled her toward the edge of the house where a narrow staircase led from the balcony to the ground.

Sage frowned, but made no effort to pull away. "Where are we going?"

"I intend to take you on a tour of the Wildlands." He led her away from the communal area into the lush vegetation of the wetlands. "It's too beautiful a day to be locked inside."

"I'm really close to a breakthrough on the scrolls," she weakly protested.

He shrugged, following the narrow path that weaved between the cypress trees.

"An hour or so away from them will help you clear your mind."

"But I thought you brought me here to decipher the scrolls?"

"I did."

"And now you want me—"

"Yes." He came to an abrupt halt, bracing Sage as she slammed into his hard body. Framing her face in his hands, he regarded her with the raw hunger that made her toes curl. "I want you." His fingers traced down her cheeks and along the line of her jaw. "Your delectable body. Your daunting brain." He offered a rueful smile. "Your wary heart."

An aching need raced through her.

She wanted to believe.

She truly did.

But...

"Lian."

He leaned down to press a tender kiss to her lips before straightening and once again grabbing her hand so he could lead her forward.

"Today, however, all I ask is that you come and play with me."

Sage swallowed a sigh.

How could she resist?

Her logic might warn she was bound to regret giving into temptation, but her heart was demanding she savor every moment she could spend with this man.

"You are a very bad influence," she muttered.

He flashed her a grin that could make her bones melt.

"Sometimes very bad can be very good."

No. Shit.

She gave up any hope of being sensible,

instead allowing herself to be led astray by her naughty cat.

"Where are we going?" she at last asked.

"Someplace my family won't find us." An edge of a growl was in his voice. "As much as I love them I'm tired of having a constant chaperone. I want to be alone with you."

With one last tug of her hand, he urged her through a swathe of Spanish moss and into a small meadow.

"Oh," she breathed, taking in the narrow channel of water that was spanned by a wooden bridge. "It's beautiful."

Lian stood at her side, his hand skimming up and down her back.

"Can you feel it?"

She tilted her head to meet his watchful gaze. "Feel what?"

"The magic."

She frowned. "I'm not Pantera."

"Just feel," he urged softly.

She parted her lips to argue, only to snap them shut as she realized that she could feel...

Something.

The warmth of the sun. The breeze that brushed her skin. The spongy ground beneath her feet.

And an unmistakable tingle that filled her body.

Easily sensing the second she accepted the truth of his words, Lian moved toward the middle of the meadow.

"Now watch," he urged.

Sage's eyes widened as a shimmering mist

suddenly surrounded Lian's large body, the air filled with a burst of heat that made her take an instinctive step backward.

Holding her breath, she pressed a hand to her heart as the mist slowly cleared to reveal a huge cat with fur as black as ebony and whiskey-gold eyes.

He was beautiful.

Proud. Powerful. Primitive.

For a breathless moment he held himself still, perhaps waiting to see if she would run away screaming in terror.

But Sage wasn't frightened.

She felt nothing but awe as she dropped to her knees and held her arms open in invitation. Slowly Lian prowled forward, nudging her with his wet nose.

Wrapping her arms around his neck, she stared directly into the eyes that held the essence of the man who'd stolen her heart.

"I see you," she whispered.

Parting his jaws, he released a roar that shook the earth.

An hour after luring Sage from her work, Lian grudgingly allowed her to leave the meadow.

As much as he was enjoying their rare time alone, he understood that his people were desperate for a way to halt Shakpi's determination to destroy them. If the scrolls had the slightest potential to offer them hope, then he couldn't allow his selfish desires to stand in the way.

And just as importantly, he understood his sweet, serious scholar.

He could momentarily distract her, but her clever mind wasn't going to be satisfied until she'd achieved the goal of translating the hieroglyphs.

It would take time to thoroughly corrupt her.

She was disappearing through the Spanish moss when a tall male with golden hair and gold eyes flecked with jade appeared from the opposite direction.

Raphael was the head of the Suits, and father to the first baby born to the Pantera in the past fifty years.

"I heard your female was a beauty, but I didn't realize she carried the gift of our ancestors."

Lian sent his friend a startled glance.

He'd been careful not to share his belief that Sage was a potential Shaman, although he was certain his family already suspected the truth.

But it was a shock that his companion had noticed from a mere glance across a meadow.

Either Raphael was a mind reader, or Sage's powers were growing now that she was in the Wildlands.

He was betting on Sage's magic becoming more pronounced.

"I suspected, but I couldn't be certain," he confessed.

The golden gaze narrowed. "Does she know?"

"She accepts that she has powers that she doesn't fully understand," he said, forcing himself not to follow as she disappeared from view.

Dammit. He'd promised he'd give her the space she needed to finish her work.

Raphael moved so he was standing directly in front of Lian, his smile wry as if he understood how difficult it was for the younger male to concentrate on anything but his mate.

"So why don't you explain it to her?"

Lian grimaced, reaching into the pocket of his jeans for the narrow leather string. He'd left his hair down because he knew that Sage enjoyed running her fingers through the long strands.

And he'd do anything to please her.

Now he wanted it out of his way.

"In the past few days I've stolen Sage from her home, placed the fate of our people on her shoulders and discovered that she's my mate. That doesn't even include being mauled by my family." He gave a short, humorless laugh, tying off the braid. "I think we can wait a few days to dump more surprises on her."

Raphael nodded, one of the few who understood. His own mate, Ashe, had gone through her own shocking transformation.

"She's stronger than you think," he assured Lian.

"I don't want her to *have* to be strong."

"Anyone who has to deal with you and your family will need a spine of steel."

Lian's lips twitched. "I suppose that's true enough," he said. He suspected that Sage was already bonding with his family, but she would have to develop well-defined boundaries if she didn't want them running her life. "Tell me what's going on."

Raphael's face hardened to a grim mask. "Mercier and Rosalie are missing."

"Fuck," Lian snarled, his gut clenching with a combination of fear and fury. As Hunters they understood that their duty was to put themselves in danger when necessary. But that knowledge didn't stop Lian from feeling a savage stab of guilt at their disappearance. "When was the last time you heard from them?"

"Yesterday morning," Raphael said. "They checked in from Dallas."

"And?"

"They said they were at the safe house and intended to return to the Wildlands last night." Raphael's eyes glowed with the power of his cat. "They never showed."

"You think our enemy has them?" he asked, even knowing the question was ridiculous.

Mercier and Rosalie would have contacted Parish if they were going to be late.

No way in hell they would just have dropped out of contact.

"What other explanation—" Raphael's words broke off on a low growl, his claws piercing his skin as a foul odor filled the meadow. "Do you smell that?"

The stench was impossible to miss.

It warned their enemies were near.

"Intruders?" he muttered, his gaze searching the shadows between the trees.

"No. Shakpi." Raphael sent him a warning frown. "Your Shaman just ran out of time."

God. Damn.

Could they just once get a break?

Lian shook his head, frustration a toxic knot in the pit of his stomach.

"The translations aren't done."

Raphael flexed his claws. "I'll try to slow her down, but we need a miracle to stop her from escaping."

There was a burst of mist and sparkling colors as Raphael shifted into a massive puma with caramel fur and golden eyes.

Lian didn't bother to watch Raphael bound across the meadow toward the cabin where they'd stashed Chayton's unconscious body.

He was already headed toward the Suits' headquarters. Once he'd checked in with Sage he would join Raphael in his battle to try and halt the goddess from escaping the Wildlands.

Reaching the large mansion he released his claws and climbed the post of the balcony. Then, vaulting over the edge of the balustrade he was bursting through the French doors.

Sage had clearly just entered the room, the white gloves dropping from her hands as she caught sight of his somber expression.

"Lian, what is it?" She crossed the floor to stand directly in front of him. "What's wrong?"

"Shakpi is awake."

She made a sound of shock, her head turning to glance toward the scrolls neatly laid out on the table.

"She can't be," she argued. "It's too soon."

"Look at me, sweetheart," he commanded, cupping her cheek with his hand and urging her back to meet his searching gaze. "Have you discovered anything that can help us?"

She bit her bottom lip. "I'm just now learning how to translate the symbols to sounds."

"What does that mean?"

"I can phonetically pronounce the glyphs, but I don't know what they mean." Distress darkened her eyes to slate. "I'm sorry. I failed you."

His brows snapped together as he wrapped her in his arms and rubbed his cheek on top of her head.

Dammit. It was bad enough he'd thrown her into the middle of their war with the evil goddess. He wouldn't have her blaming herself for something that wasn't her fault. Especially when he was the one who'd lured her away from her work.

"Don't say that," he chided. "Even if Shakpi escapes, these scrolls might help us prepare our defenses." Lifting his head, he peered down at her pale face. "We need you, Dr. Parker."

She gave a small nod, then abruptly

wrinkled her nose as a blast of putrid air swept through the open French doors.

"Good lord, what is that?" she muttered.

Grabbing Sage's arm, he gave her a push toward the far door. "Run."

"What?" She dug in her heels, looking at him as if he'd lost his mind.

She wasn't wrong.

The mere thought that Shakpi was headed in this direction was enough to send him over the edge.

The evil bitch was supposed to be trying to escape.

It's what she'd done the first time they'd tried to hold her captive.

Snatching the phone from his pocket, he sent a quick message to his mother.

"Go to my family," he rasped. "They'll take you back to your home."

She was shaking her head before he ever finished speaking. "No, I'm not leaving you."

He glanced over his shoulder, a shudder of revulsion wracking his body as Shakpi reached the edge of the clearing.

"Don't be stubborn." He jerked his attention back to the female who was making his heart squeeze with terror. He could face a thousand crazy-ass goddesses before he could contemplate the thought of Sage in danger for even a second. "There's nothing you can do here."

Her chin tilted. "I'm not helpless."

He fisted his hands. Where the hell was this coming from?

He was impulsive and always ready to dive into danger headfirst. Sage was supposed to be the sensible, cautious, blessedly logical one.

"You can't stop a goddess," he pointed out in rough tones.

She remained stubbornly in place. "Can you?"

"Sage."

Without warning, she moved forward, going on her tiptoes to press a kiss to his lips.

It was a gentle caress laced with the promise of a future.

Oh...hell.

"You do what you do and let me do what I do," she commanded in soft tones.

In that second, she could have ordered him to stop the world from turning and he'd have done everything in his power to fulfill her wish.

Accepting he'd lost this particular battle, he turned to run out of room, shifting into his cat as he sailed over the railing of the balcony and prepared to battle a goddess.

CHAPTER 7

Sage ran her fingers over the glyphs, desperately trying to ignore the vicious roars and occasional snarls of pain that filled the air.

She didn't have claws or teeth. Or even a damned gun.

For now, the only way to help Lian was by concentrating on the scrolls.

She was so close, the symbols forming into words in her head as a tingle of power raced through her blood.

This wasn't a history of the Pantera as she'd first assumed. Or even a detailed explanation of how to destroy Shakpi as Lian had hoped.

This was...magic.

Lost in her thoughts, Sage didn't sense the approaching man until he lightly tapped on her shoulder.

She jerked her head around to discover a tall man with milky brown skin, blue eyes and dark hair that was closely buzzed to his scalp.

Xavier was the Geek she'd been in cyber contact with for the past four years. Of course, she'd assumed he was another researcher, not a mythical puma shifter.

"What are you doing?" the man snapped, his expression grim as he towered over her. "You need to evacuate."

"No." She turned back to the scrolls to point toward a hieroglyph shaped like a bluebird. "What does the word Hielar mean?"

With an effort, Xavier leashed his obvious desire to be in the clearing below with his pack mates.

"Hielar?" His brow furrowed as he searched his mind for the answer. "In the old language it meant 'come.'"

Sage felt a flicker of hope.

Was it possible she was on the right track?

"Come or summon?" she demanded.

"What are you suggesting?"

"I think this is a spell."

Xavier stiffened, suddenly offering her his full attention. "A spell to get rid of Shakpi?"

She gave a shake of her head. "No. To summon someone." She bit her bottom lip, touching her fingers to the glyphs. The strange prickles continued to race through her body, as if urging her to speak the words, but the symbols remained frustratingly out of focus. "Or something."

"Dammit." Xavier glared at the scrolls in frustration. "I was so certain these could help."

"I think they can," she insisted.

He shook his head. "Dr. Parker, I appreciate you traveling here and trying to decipher the scrolls, but the last thing we want is to risk summoning some unknown spirit."

She flinched as she heard a heavy body crash into a tree below.

She was a scientist at heart. The sort of person who depended on logic and fact. Which was why she'd tried to suppress the magic that bubbled deep inside her for so long.

Since arriving in the Wildlands, however, she'd allowed herself to lower her barriers and 'see' the scrolls with her emotions, not the eyes of a researcher.

At the beginning she'd thought she'd sensed the lingering echo of the goddess because she assumed Opela had written the scroll.

Now that she realized it was a spell...

Well, the only reasonable explanation was that it was meant to summon the elusive goddess.

"Even a spirit that has the same power as Shakpi?" she asked.

Xavier made a sound of impatience. "There isn't any."

"Her sister."

Not surprisingly, the large male glared at her as if she'd just committed sacrilege. Even though it'd been centuries since Opela had disappeared from the Wildlands, the Pantera deeply mourned her loss.

"Opela sacrificed herself to imprison Shakpi," he said in harsh tones.

Sage reached out to lightly touch his arm.

She didn't mean to offend Xavier, but she didn't have time to do this in a more diplomatic way.

"You don't truly believe she's gone," she insisted.

He scowled, no doubt assuming she was arguing semantics. "Not completely gone, but—"

A loud yelp sounded from below. Lian. Sage pressed a hand to her heart. She could physically feel his pain.

"Oh hell," she breathed, sending Xavier a pleading glance. "We have to do something."

He hesitated for less than a heartbeat before giving a sharp nod of his head.

"Say the spell."

That wasn't what Sage had been expecting.

"Me?" She blinked in confusion. "I'm not Pantera."

"You have the magic," he told her, his gaze boring into her with a fierce determination. "You're the only one who does."

She stepped away, wrapping her arms around her waist.

It was one thing to be asked to translate the scrolls. She had full faith in her abilities to decipher even the most obscure languages.

But what did she know about magic?

A big fat nothing.

"What makes you think I can cast a spell?" she rasped.

His huge body vibrated with the need to join the battle, but easily sensing her rising panic, he reached to grasp her upper arms in a light grip.

"Do you remember the first time we met?"

She licked her dry lips. "In the chat room?"

"Yes, I sent a fellow Pantera a message in our private language. Imagine my shock when you managed to translate it."

The internet chat rooms she'd discovered after becoming an adjunct professor had proven to be a godsend.

She might be too introverted to mix easily with people in public, but she'd been astonishingly capable of joining in the numerous debates and scholarly exchanges in the various rooms.

"I thought it was a brainteaser," she confessed, easily recalling the strange conversation that had popped up on her screen. It'd taken her several hours, but she'd eventually worked out the basic construct of the unknown words and sent a message back to Xavier in the same language. "But a talent for translations doesn't equate to mystic abilities."

"No, but over the years I sent you more and more obscure texts, most of which were nothing but gibberish to me."

She arched her brows. "Were they Pantera texts?"

He shook his head. "They'd been written by a Shaman."

"Oh." Suddenly she realized that this man had been subtly testing her over the years. He'd suspected all along that there was more to her than just another scholar. "That's why you had me brought here."

"I'd hoped you could decipher the scrolls. I didn't know they were a spell," he readily confessed, his fingers tightening on her arms. "Will you help?"

What could she say? She didn't know how or when it'd happened, but she knew with absolute clarity that Lian was now the most important thing in her world. She would give her life to protect him.

"I'll try."

"That's all we can ask." His eyes glowed with a lethal lust for blood as his cat broke free of its leash. "I have to go," he growled, already shifting into a huge black puma before he was pouncing across the balcony and over the railing.

Savagely squashing the need to follow behind Xavier, Sage instead turned to place her hand flat on the scrolls.

This was how she could help.

She couldn't allow herself to be distracted.

"Okay, Sage, you can do this," she muttered. "Lian needs you."

Emptying her thoughts of everything except the hieroglyphs, she allowed the magic to flow through her blood and softly spoke the words that felt like fire on her lips.

It took several minutes to complete the entire spell that was spread over five scrolls, but reaching the last glyph, she straightened from the table and sucked in a deep breath.

She didn't know what she'd expected.

Lightning. Earthquakes.

The sky falling.

Instead, she smelled...fresh grass as a misty shape formed and floated out the French doors.

Was that the goddess?

With a shake of her head, Sage was headed toward the door. She'd done everything possible with the scrolls.

Now she intended to be with Lian.

They would face the danger together.

Lian snarled as he watched the tall man with a lean face and dark hair braided down his back raise his hand. Chayton, the one-time Shaman, was looking decidedly worse for wear with deep claw marks down one side of his face, and a bloody nose. But while his body was human, he was infected by the spirit of the goddess who had the sort of magic that was making it impossible for the gathering Pantera to completely halt his progress across the large clearing.

To prove his point, the man released a bolt of energy that slammed into the charging golden puma.

With a pained yip, Raphael was tossed into a nearby tree, the crunch of bones making Lian wince.

Shit.

Even in his puma form, he understood that things weren't going well. Unfortunately, they didn't have any choice but to try and keep the spirit contained in the Wildlands. If Shakpi managed to get past their borders she would disappear and they would once again be under constant threat of attack.

There was a blur of black as Xavier leapt through the air and hit Chayton from behind. The Shaman muttered a curse before he reached over his shoulder and blasted the clinging puma with enough force to knock Xavier unconscious.

Ignoring his shattered ribs and painful wounds that had been scorched into his flesh, Lian leaped forward, his jaws wide as he went directly for Chayton's throat.

He managed to get close enough to scrape his elongated canines across the bastard's shoulder, but before he could latch onto the flesh, he felt fingers close around his neck to bring him to an abrupt halt.

With an inhuman strength, Shakpi held him off the ground, studying him with glowing eyes.

"Why do you fight me?" the goddess demanded, an unmistakable frustration etched onto the lean, bloody face. "You can't possibly win."

Lian shifted to his human form, using the abrupt change to free himself from the brutal grip.

"Not alone," he snarled, backing toward the edge of the clearing. Maybe if he could piss her off enough, he could lure the evil bitch away from his people. "But we are pack. You can't defeat us all."

"I don't need to defeat all of you." A smug smile touched Chayton's lips. "Just one."

"One..." Realization smacked into Lian. Shakpi wasn't trying to escape the Wildlands, because she was convinced that the key to her ultimate destruction of the Pantera was the child. "Raphael," he shouted toward the golden puma slowly rising to his feet. "She's after Soyala."

Raphael's roar made the trees tremble as he raced across the grass to the house he shared with his mate.

At the same time, Lian was charging forward to halt Shakpi as she tried to follow the fleeing puma.

He wrapped his arms around Chayton's slender body, intending to knock him to the ground. But clearly tired of playing with him, the goddess pushed him away with a jolt of her power.

"No, nothing can stop me now."

Instantly Lian's entire body was filled with a shocking pain that forced his heart to a shuddering halt and wrenched the air from his lungs.

Fuck.

He was going to die.

There was no way to survive the massive injuries to his inner organs.

The thought had barely formed when the enticing scent of lemon teased its way past the fog in his mind.

No.

He wasn't going to give up.

Not when Sage needed him.

With a groan of agony, he opened his swollen eyes, discovering Shakpi standing over him.

"Why?" He forced the question past his numb lips. "Why do you hate us?"

The glowing eyes filled with envy. "You are an abomination."

The goddess truly was mad, Lian acknowledged in horror.

"We're the children of Opela," he ground out.

"She should never have created you. It was a mistake."

"She loves us."

"No. She loves me." With a burst of fury, Shakpi reached down to grab Lian by the throat, yanking him back to his feet. "She promised to love me."

"And I do," a soft, lyrical voice said.

The fingers on Lian's neck tightened as the goddess turned to study the small cloud of mist that hovered a few feet away.

"Opela?"

"It is I, sister." The soft voice came from the mist that shimmered in the late afternoon sunlight, the air suddenly filled with the scent of fresh grass. "What have you done?"

Lian blinked in confusion.

Could this truly be Opela?

It was certainly as good an explanation as any other.

Awe spread through Lian even as he struggled against the shattering pain.

"Release him, Shakpi," the female voice commanded.

Shakpi shook her head. "This is a trick."

"No trick." The scent of grass thickened even as the misty shape floated closer. "I've come for you."

The hand that was squeezing Lian's throat eased, as the goddess concentrated on the shadowed form standing directly in front of them.

"You tried to destroy me."

Lian could actually feel the sorrow that pulsed from Opela. "I would never wish to hurt you, my sister."

"You locked me away," Shakpi hissed, the earth quaking beneath her remembered sense of betrayal.

"I couldn't allow you to attack my children."

"You should never have created them." Shakpi glanced toward Lian, her eyes filled with hate. "They took you away from me."

"I have always been here for you." The mist swirled, expanding to touch Shakpi.

The evil goddess dropped her hand from Lian, but not before he felt the sheer love that was gently wrapping around her.

A love that was as vast as the universe.

"You left and I was alone," Shakpi whispered.

"Come with me, sister."

Shakpi shook her head. "I won't return to the prison."

"Let's go home," the female voice gently urged.

The lean face softened with a yearning that came from the very soul.

"Home? You swear?"

"Yes, Shakpi. It's time."

Chayton's body trembled and then collapsed as the dark shadow of Shakpi's spirit left The Shaman's body to join with her sister.

Barely capable of standing, Lian dropped to his knees, instinctively reaching to feel for Chayton's pulse before he glanced up at the mist that now shimmered with a dazzling display of color.

"You're leaving?"

He felt something like the brush of a finger over his swollen cheek, offering a warmth that seared away the most grievous of his injuries.

"It's for the best, my child."

"But you just returned."

His heart twisted with regret. To be surrounded by her gentle glory was going to be a memory he would never forget.

"I've been here, Lian, just as I always will be," she promised in musical tones. "The Wildlands are a part of me." There was another burst of color from the mist. "And a part of Shakpi. Life and death. Night and day."

He battled the darkness that was threatening. Even with Opela's healing he remained painfully weakened from his battle.

"What about the magic?" he demanded, unable to believe their struggles were over.

"It's in the land and in you, but the source now rests in the child." There was a hint of warning in her voice. "Guard her well."

"Yes," he murmured, a sense of pleasure filling his heart as the scent of lemons surrounded him.

A second later, Sage was kneeling beside him, her arm wrapping around his shoulders.

The mist began to fade, but before it completely disappeared, Opela's voice whispered on the breeze.

"Welcome home, Sage."

Chapter 8

The private room at the back of the clinic that was reserved for patients who were hurt, but capable of healing on their own, was big enough to hold a large, comfortable bed and two leather seats for visitors.

It wasn't, however, large enough to contain a dozen full-grown Pantera who were determined to fuss over the man who was lying on the mattress with his ribs bandaged and healing herbs rubbed onto the burns that marred his upper arm.

Sage hovered next to the heavy walnut headboard, needing to be near Lian, but understanding his family were anxious to assure themselves he was going to make a full recovery.

Enduring the avalanche of concern for nearly an hour, Lian at last reached his breaking point when his grandmother decided she would comb and braid his hair.

"That's it. Everyone out," he roared, pointing to the door. There was a shocked silence as the visitors stared at Lian with wide eyes, then with a sudden smile Lian's father was firmly ushering the crowd out of the room. Prepared to follow, Sage had barely moved when slender fingers wrapped around her wrist. "Not you," Lian growled. "You stay."

She arched her brows, hiding her flare of relief.

When she'd seen Lian kneeling on the ground with his face swollen and covered in blood she'd been terrified he was dying.

Even now she felt compelled to reach out and brush her fingers down his cheek to convince herself he was alive and well.

"Bossy," she murmured.

"Frustrated," he corrected. Pulling up the sheet that covered his naked body he sent her a smile of smoldering invitation. "Join me."

Her heart jolted with instant arousal. Just being near Lian was enough to make her pulse race and her stomach clench with excitement.

To have a full view of all that bronzed deliciousness...

It was enough to make any female tingle in anticipation.

But she hadn't forgotten that he'd just had the shit beat out of him by a crazed goddess.

The last thing she wanted was for him to interrupt his healing.

"You're hurt," she forced herself to say.

He shrugged. "I'll feel better once I have my mate next to me."

Her breath caught at his blunt words. "Mate?"

He studied her pale face, his body tensing as he searched for her reaction.

"Does that frighten you?"

Barely aware she was moving, Sage crawled onto the bed and allowed Lian to wrap her in his waiting arms.

It wasn't just that she sensed his need to feel her pressed against him, but his question had touched her most vulnerable nerve.

She *was* frightened.

Not at the thought of being this man's mate.

Every part of her desperately longed to believe that they were destined to be together.

But she'd been taught that she couldn't depend on love. Not when it could be so easily snatched away.

Trust wasn't easy for her to offer.

"How can you be sure?" she demanded, burrowing against his warm body as his intoxicating musk saturated her senses. "You barely know me."

His hand slid beneath her sweatshirt to stroke a soothing path up and down her back.

"My cat decided the moment he saw you," he told her, his lips brushing her temple. "The human side wasn't far behind."

Her fingers unconsciously stroked over the hard muscles of his chest, seeking reassurance in his solid strength.

"What if you grow tired of me?"

"Tired?" Lian gave an unexpected chuckle, tugging the sweatshirt over her head and tossing it onto the floor. "Impossible."

"Lian—"

Her words were forgotten as Lian methodically stripped away the rest of her clothes with heart-jolting impatience.

"No, it truly is impossible," he assured her, his tone absent as his gaze surveyed her naked body with a hungry urgency. "Pantera mate for life. There will never be another for me."

Sage felt her pussy clench in need, the damp heat filling the air with the scent of her arousal.

She struggled to concentrate on her point.

She did have a point, didn't she?

She groaned as his fingers skimmed down her stomach, heading for the aching void between her legs.

"I'm not Pantera." She managed to grasp the unraveling threads of her argument.

"You belong to us." His lips nuzzled over her cheek to the corner of her mouth. "To me."

He lifted his head to reveal eyes that glowed with the raw need of his cat.

The same need that was churning through her.

"Belong?" she tried to chide, only to have the word come out as a groan.

He nipped her lower lip. "Just as I belong to you." He kissed her with a slow, thorough brand of possession. "Forever." He nibbled a path of destruction down the curve of her neck. "Stay, Dr. Parker. Be my mate and our Shaman."

She braced herself for another surge of fear, but instead, a sense of...rightness settled in her heart.

Lian wasn't her parents.

He was loyal and supportive, and lethally charming.

Precisely the sort of male to teach an aging spinster how to enjoy her life.

Sage, however, wasn't yet entirely convinced she was a mystical Shaman.

"I don't even know what a Shaman is supposed to do," she protested.

His finger slid between her slick folds, a smile of satisfaction curving his lips as she instinctively lifted her hips in response to his intimate caress.

"Each has their own skills," he explained. "But most have been able to sense the faction of a newborn Pantera."

"Faction?" The question came out as a squeak as his finger slid into her tight channel, sending shockwaves of pleasure through her body.

His teeth toyed with the lobe of her ear, the hard length of his cock pressed against her hip.

"If they're destined to be a Hunter or a Diplomat or a Healer."

That sounded...

His thumb found her sensitive clit, circling it with teasing strokes.

"Oh."

"They can also decipher messages from the ancestors."

He kissed his way to the curve of her breast, latching onto the aching tip with an urgency that made her whimper.

"Lian." Sage threaded her fingers through the dark strands of his hair.

"Hmm?"

Her back arched, bliss shuddering through her as his finger thrust in and out of her body with a growing insistence.

"We're having a conversation."

He lifted his head, his bronzed features tight with the strain of leashing his desire.

"The only thing I want to discuss is our mating."

A rueful smile curved her lips.

For years she'd hidden away from the world, trying to hide her abilities as if they were something shameful.

It'd taken a puma shifter to teach her that her gifts were special.

And so was she.

"You're pushing," she teased, lifting her head to steal a quick kiss.

His eyes were molten gold as he stared down at her with a somber expression.

"I know," he said, his voice husky with emotion. "I've claimed your body. Let me claim your heart, Dr. Parker."

She framed his beautiful face in her hands, smiling with sheer joy.

"You already have."

Heat licked over her skin as the power of his cat blasted through the air.

"Is that a yes?" he growled.

Sage didn't hesitate.

She'd felt alone her entire life.

Now she not only had a mate, but an entire family who were anxious to make her feel at home.

"That's a definite yes."

He didn't give her the opportunity for second thoughts.

With his cat shimmering in his eyes, he swiped his hand over her lower stomach, the claws slicing through her flesh.

Sage gasped, but shockingly, there was no pain, only pleasure as he swooped his head down to claim her lips in a kiss that made her toes curl in pleasure.

"Mine," he growled, rolling on top of her to settle between her spread legs.

Then, sliding his cock deep inside her body, he physically connected them even as their souls entwined to become one.

EPILOGUE

Lian heaved a sated sigh as Sage ran a brush through his hair.

He'd protested when she'd pulled on her clothes and grabbed the brush his grandmother had left behind. He wanted another few hours of having her naked and sweaty beneath him, but he couldn't argue with her point that the clinic wasn't the most private place to indulge his endless lust for his mate.

In a few hours the Healers would be satisfied he was strong enough to leave and he intended to choose one of the empty cabins that was on the opposite side of the Wildlands from his family home.

Once he had Sage alone he was going to lock the door and throw away the key.

Until then he had to be satisfied with the feel of her hands running through his hair as she pulled it into a braid.

Savoring her soft touch and the lemony scent that clung to his skin, Lian scowled as a sharp knock intruded into their peaceful silence.

"Go away," he snapped.

The door was shoved open to reveal Raphael, who was dressed in jeans and a T-shirt despite the fact his wounds hadn't fully healed.

Lian tensed, a sudden anger racing through him as he caught sight of the male's bleak expression.

Dammit.

They'd just survived yet another attempt by Shakpi to commit genocide.

Hadn't they earned a few centuries of peace and quiet?

"I have news," the leader of the Suits announced.

"Do you want me to leave?" Sage asked, already moving off the bed.

"No, you're pack now." Lian wrapped an arm around her shoulder and pulled her tight against his side. "Our business is your business."

She stiffened, as if waiting for Raphael to deny her right to be at Lian's side.

Of course he didn't.

Sage was pack.

"He's right," Raphael said with a simple honesty. "You belong to us."

Feeling Sage relax against his side, Lian focused his attention on his friend.

"What's wrong?"

"We had word from Mercier and Rosalie's kidnappers."

A growl rumbled in Lian's chest.

So they had been taken by the enemy.

"Bastards," he ground out. "Did you inform them that their goddess has abandoned them?"

"Yes."

Lian narrowed his eyes. "And?"

A sudden heat filled the air as Raphael struggled to contain his fury.

"And their demands have nothing to do with Shakpi."

"Then what the hell do they want?" Lian asked. Without their evil goddess to give them a purpose, he'd expected them to slink into the shadows. "Money?"

"No." Raphael's expression was hard as stone. "An exchange for one of our prisoners."

An icy chill of premonition inched down Lian's spine.

"Who?"

Raphael clenched his hands, the name coming out like a curse.

"Hiss."

Other Books by Alexandra Ivy

Guardians of Eternity
Hunt the Darkness
Darkness Avenged
Levet
Fear the Darkness
Bound by Darkness
The Real Werewives of Vampire County
Supernatural
Yours for Eternity
Devoured by Darkness
Beyond the Darkness
Darkness Unleashed
Darkness Revealed
Darkness Everlasting
Embrace the Darkness
When Darkness Comes

Immortal Rogues Series
** Please note this series is a reprint from the 2003
Historical Vampire Series written as Deborah Raleigh **
My Lord Vampire (#1)
My Lord Eternity (#2)
My Lord Immortality (#3)

Sentinel Series
Predatory — Sentinel Anthology
Born in Blood (#1)

Bayou Heat Series
Raphael & Parish (1 & 2)
Bayon & Jean-Baptiste (3 & 4)
Talon & Xavier (5 & 6)
Sebastian & Aristide (7 & 8)

Rapture Series
Sinful Rapture
First Rapture
Wicked Firsts

About the Author

Alexandra Ivy is a *New York Times* and *USA Today* bestselling author of the Guardians of Eternity series, as well as the Sentinels and Bayou Heat that she writes with Laura Wright. After majoring in theatre she decided she prefers to bring her characters to life on paper rather than stage. She lives in Missouri with her family. Visit her website at alexandraivy.com.

ROCH

LAURA WRIGHT

CHAPTER 1

After a quick shift from puma to Pantera, Roch stood on the dirt path outside Medical and slid the knot of his wrinkled tie into place.

"Isn't that the same suit you had on last night, brother?" Damien asked, his black eyes heavy with amusement.

Roch regarded his friend and colleague. "Yes, it is." He didn't like it, but time demanded it be so. The position of Diplomat deserved the respect of a suit—even if that suit was rumpled and carried the faint scent of a night gone awry.

As a morning breeze off the bayou moved over them, the tall, black-haired male chuckled. "You're such a manwhore, you know that?"

"Don't insult me, Damien," Roch said, running his fingers through his thick, disheveled blond hair. He was never sleeping on a couch again. No matter what the circumstance.

"What? By calling you a whore?"

"No. By calling me a man." Roch turned his

ice blue gaze on his fellow Suit. His brows lifted a fraction of an inch. "Besides, nothing happened with the female."

The male snorted. "Yeah, I believe that. Remember, I know you. Have seen how the females respond to you. It's unfair as hell." He paused to wave to a couple of female Hunters passing by. When they barely gave him a second glance, he turned his attention back to Roch, his expression hopeful. "Teach me."

Roch cracked a dry smile. Damien was a good male; funny, honest and loyal. Not to mention a brilliant Diplomat. But this understanding of his, this belief that Roch possessed some kind of sexual magic, or— pardon the phrase—catnip with the females he encountered was complete bullshit. All he had was an open and respectful desire. And maybe the belief that a female's pleasure came before his own.

"I saw you leave The Cougar's Den with her," Damien pointed out. "And you show up this morning in the same clothes, looking like you hardly slept." He grinned. "That's what I call a successful night."

Roch growled softly with impatience. The night before had been anything but successful. In fact, it had been pretty much hell. Owning to it wasn't high on his priority list, but he knew Damien wouldn't stop questioning him until he was tossed a little something to satisfy his curiosity.

"The female is getting married in a week," Roch said, wishing he'd had time to stop home for a shower. No matter how he tried to play this, Raphael and the other Suits were going to give him some serious shit about the wrinkled jacket and pants—not to mention the lingering odors of alcohol and a pissed-off stomach.

Damien looked genuinely confused. "So she's getting married. And?"

"I don't play with claimed females, Damien."

The confusion on the male's face deepened. "Then what did you do last night?"

Her roommate.

Roch grinned at that. At his foolish, yet highly decadent thoughts. It had been the plan. He'd even agreed to let the engaged human female watch—which she'd been damn keen on doing. But then hell had pulled him under, shaking and churning his guts until he'd become violently ill. First all over the white sheepskin rug on their living room floor, then in the bathroom for a good two hours. He'd passed out on their couch shortly after, like a hammered teenager.

Granted, Pantera had their share of medical issues to deal with, but stomach sickness was a rarity. He'd woken up late and apologized profusely to the women. And on his way back to the bayou, he had called to arrange for a new rug to be delivered and maid service to come to their apartment.

"Forget last night," Roch said, motioning for Damien to follow as he headed toward the doors of Medical. "Today is what matters. And the work ahead. But I will say that Hiss had better give us the answers we're looking for. My cat is just aching to attack something."

"Hiss?" Damien repeated, his brows slamming together in confusion. "Is that who we're meeting with this morning?"

"You didn't know?"

The male shook his head. "Didn't know who we're meeting, and sure as hell didn't know he'd been brought to Medical."

A flicker of unease moved through Roch. It wasn't like the leader of the Suits to keep information from his faction members. "I'm sure Raphael meant to inform you."

"Maybe he doesn't trust me."

The bitterness in Damien's voice wasn't hard to miss. It was difficult being the newest member of any faction, but with the Diplomats it was doubly so. There was so much information, so much protocol—so many secrets that needed to be kept to protect the Pantera.

"Why would you think that?" Roch asked him.

The male shrugged. "Hiss was a friend back when we were cubs."

With a sniff of amusement, Roch yanked the door wide. "Hiss had many friends. Raphael is no doubt suffering from intense stress due to Shakpi's dramatic departure, and that we've been outed to the humans—and then there's the lack of sleep due to the incessant squawk of one called Soyala."

That seemed to both smooth the male's raised hackles and cause him to grin. "The cub. I'm sure he doesn't mind her cries. A young is a great blessing to a male."

"To some males, that's true," Roch answered. "I, however, prefer work—and the cries of a male who's just come clean after a particularly rough interrogation."

Damien laughed. "So, why was Hiss brought here?"

"They're testing him," Roch said as they moved down the hall. "His blood, heart, mind—even his cat. While his tongue remains quiet, the Nurturers are hoping to glean some information as to why our new enemies would trade two Pantera for one. Why Hiss is so important to them."

"I still think loyalty to these humans could be a factor," Damien put in, giving a quick smile to a passing female who was in her puma state. "Maybe they have a long history. Maybe they consider Hiss one of their own. And the exchange for Rosalie and Mercier is their way of demonstrating that."

Medical was alive with activity, as it always was in the morning hours. Roch spotted Raphael up ahead. The leader of the Diplomatic Faction was dressed sharply in a tailored black suit and was speaking intently to one of the head Nurturers, Jean-Baptiste.

"Well, they can have him," Roch said with a growl. "As soon as he tells us everything he knows, and we have our loyal Pantera back again."

A few feet from his boss, Roch gritted his teeth as his stomach rolled hard and fast again. What the hell was going on with him? Bad alcohol? Bad food? What? And why was it still affecting him? As he neared the two Pantera, he shoved the feeling back. He didn't have time for ailments. He had a job to do. And, he mused with a forced grin, the cries of a traitor male to elicit.

Fired.

FIRED!?!

Lydia Page stared at the trees swaying in the breeze outside the picture window and wondered why she hadn't anticipated the reaction from the partners at her law firm. Maybe because they were both women, and had children of their own? Of course, they also had husbands and nannies to go along with those children. But surely they understood that she'd be committed to the firm even if she had a child?

Nope.

To be fair, they hadn't said they were firing her because of her pregnancy. Because, you know, that would be highly illegal. Instead, they'd claimed they were firing her for excessive absences. Which was such crap. With the illness and subsequent death of her mother six months ago, she'd taken some time off. Two days over her allotment, to be specific—two days both partners had verbally agreed to. But as a lawyer, she knew how well oral agreements stood up, and how quickly they were forgotten.

Behind her, the office door opened. "Ms. Page," came the doctor's voice. "Thank you for coming in today."

"Of course," she said.

It was this very lunchtime appointment at The Haymore Center that her assistant had both scheduled and shared with one of the partners' assistants a few days ago. Clearly, the partners didn't believe that a single mother could put in the kind of hours they wanted.

Well, screw them, Lydia thought, her eyes now set on the doctor seated across from her. She could get another job. Hell, maybe she'd even open her own practice.

"How are you today, Ms. Page?" the doctor inquired, his gaze trained on the paperwork before him on the desk.

"Fine," she said brightly. "No morning sickness yet. But I'm sure that will come. My mom was really sick with me from six weeks to four months. Barfing all the time." She smiled and touched her flat belly. "But what's a little barf when you get something so precious at the end of it, right?" She laughed softly.

The doctor took a deep breath and let it out slowly. "Ms. Page, I'd like to discuss your blood test and ultrasound results."

It was then that he looked up from his paperwork and met her gaze. His eyes were a cold brown and deep set. His mouth a thin, tense line. Lydia felt the blood drain from her face, and her heart start to pound. "What's wrong? The baby—"

"The baby looks fine," he said evenly. "Healthy."

"Oh my god." She put a hand to her chest. "Oh, thank goodness. I—"

"But there is something we need to talk about," he amended.

The relief from a moment ago evaporated and heat prickled through her. "What?"

"The embryo's development is further along than it should be." His tone was unsympathetic at best.

Lydia's hands started to tremble. "What does that mean? How far along is it?"

"The fetus should be measuring four weeks. But instead, it's twelve."

Lydia stared at him, her heart beating so fast now it actually hurt. She'd only met Dr. Ambrose twice. Once for a consult, and the second time when he performed the insemination. The man was purported to be a genius so she had overlooked his lack of warmth and bedside manner. With the job she'd hired him to do, skill was far more important than kindness. But right then, staring at him across his desk, feeling as though she might implode from fear and grief, she wouldn't have minded a little bit of gentleness.

"What does this mean?" she asked in a near whisper. "And why did it happen?" *My baby*...

Once again, the door opened behind her and a woman's voice called out, "Knock, knock."

"Come in, Erin," the doctor said in a grave

tone, avoiding Lydia's gaze as much as possible now.

The woman strode past Lydia and came to stand beside the doctor. She was somewhere in her mid-thirties, with pale brown hair and dark, intelligent eyes. She looked from Lydia to the doctor, then back again. "I see you've been told."

Her words were meant to sound sympathetic, but they came out detached and clinical. Lydia clasped her hands together. Her palms were cold and wet. "Yes," she said.

"I am sorry, Ms. Page," she said, handing Lydia a document. "But I'm sure you understand why it's imperative that you terminate this pregnancy immediately."

CHAPTER 2

"I've told Raphael and now I'll tell you," Hiss growled. "The only Pantera I will speak to are the elders."

The Hunter could be damn intimidating, even strapped down to a bed with needles sticking out of his arms. Though he felt like shit, Roch stood imposingly over the male, arms crossed over his chest. "You think you're in any position to make demands, traitor?"

"Yes, I believe I am."

"Arrogance won't get you anywhere but back in a cell," Roch threatened.

"The elders will never come here," Damien put in from his position at the foot of the bed. "So just do us all a favor and end this. Tell us why these humans want you."

"I don't know," he ground out, his dark grey eyes narrowing with hatred.

"Bullshit," Damien growled.

"Give us names, addresses and plans," Roch said calmly. "And we'll return you to your humans."

Hiss's lip curled. "They're not *my* humans, asshole. They're not my anything. I don't know them. My dealings were with the followers of Shakpi. And whatever I did, whoever I used, it was for myself and my family alone. Not for some human cause."

"Maybe we should bring Reny here," Roch suggested, watching to see if the male's cat flashed behind his eyes. It didn't. It hadn't in quite some time. "Let the long-lost sister have a visit with her traitor brother. Have a nice familial heart-to-heart."

"Fuck you," Hiss ground out.

Roch leaned in, bile forming in his throat. "No. Fuck you. No matter what your reasons for doing what you did, they weren't good enough. You screwed your kind, your blood. You have forced us out of hiding. You have created fear in the hearts of our females. Including your sister." Concerned that he could vomit on the male with all the seizing up going on inside his belly, he stood up again. "You know they have Rosalie, right?"

Hiss's expression turned pained. "Yes, I know."

"She's a good friend of yours, isn't she?"

This time Hiss didn't answer. He turned away.

"You know what, you don't even deserve to breathe, you—oh, fuck me—" Roch sucked in air, his legs threatening to buckle. A wave of dizziness was moving over and through him. If he remained, he was going to lose his shit. He pushed away from the bed and growled to his colleague. "Take over, Damien."

"Hey," the male called after him as he headed for the door. "You all right?"

"Just keep at it," Roch ground out. "I'll inform Raphael."

He stumbled out into the hallway. This was bullshit. Whatever was going on with him. He didn't do sickness. He didn't accept anything that pulled him away from his work. His cat scratched at his insides as he walked down the hall. The thing wanted out. No. It wanted to take over. It knew his male form was weak, and this scratching, pawing—it was a protective instinct.

"What the hell's wrong with you?"

Roch gave Raphael a quick nod as the male fell into step beside him. "Just something I ate." *Or drank. Or came into contact with. Or...who the hell knows.*

"You look like shit," the leader of the Suits remarked. "Come to think of it, you looked like shit when you got here. You should go get checked out."

"No," Roch said quickly and gruffly.

"Come on, brother. Jean-Baptiste can take a quick look. Or if you want a female, Doc Julia—"

"I said I'm fine." Roch picked up the pace. He needed to get outside. Air. Sun. His puma. A Pantera's digestive system was quick to flush out anything it didn't like, so whatever was going on with him should pass in a few hours. "I'm going home."

Raphael continued to follow him. "Are you sure you can make it on your own?"

The growl Roch tossed the male's way ended the question and answer session. But it also stole some of Roch's strength. "I left Damien with Hiss..." he managed to mutter before he hit the glass doors.

"Fine. Just go," Raphael called after him. "I got this."

Roch burst through the doors, and the second the sunshine hit his skin and the breeze of the bayou entered his nostrils, his cat took over. It was as though his male form melted into his puma, and he instantly felt strong and healthy.

With a quick snarl at the surrounding Pantera who were heading for the bayou and midday meal, Roch took off. For the forest, and for the border of the Wildlands—so sure about what he had to do next, he didn't question it.

After all, he was pure instinct.

"The baby will have defects, right?" Lydia said before the woman, Erin, could utter another word or thrust a pen her way. "That's what you're telling me? It may be born with a deformity." She tossed the papers on the doctor's desk. "Well, let me say I don't care. I don't care. This is my child."

Erin turned to the doctor and raised her eyebrows. Clearly, she wasn't expecting such a response. Well, she could just suck it. Her heart slamming against her ribs, Lydia inched forward on her chair and fought for a serious, businesslike expression. "I'm not going to sue anyone, if that's what you're worried about. I knew the risks when I had the procedure."

"Legal action isn't what we're concerned about, Ms. Page," the doctor put in.

Yes," Erin agreed. "As you said, you knew the risks, and you did sign a contract—"

"Then what else is there?" Lydia interrupted. "Look, there's got to be some chance. I'm sure you've seen situations like this before. Isn't it at all possible that the baby could turn out to be normal?"

"Normal?" Erin repeated, then sniffed as if she scented something vile. "No."

Tears pricked Lydia's eyes.

"We'd like to take care of this today, Ms. Page," the doctor stated.

"No," Lydia said. This was ridiculous. Why were they pushing her? Why weren't they at least letting her think? Have some time—

"We need you to trust us," Erin put in, her tone strangely calm.

"I told you, I'm not getting rid of the baby."

"It isn't safe," the doctor pressed.

"I'll take that risk."

The doctor sat back in his chair. "You'll be a pariah and your child will be a freak. Is that what you want?"

Lydia's heart stopped. Or that's what it felt like. Cold, alone, disgusted. Her hands shaking slightly, she stood up.

"What are you doing, Ms. Page?" Erin asked warily.

"Leaving," Lydia informed her. "And I won't be coming back."

The doctor cursed softly. Erin, however, wasn't giving up. "Wait. Please. The donor you chose—"

Lydia swung her purse over her shoulder. "What about him?"

The woman glanced at the doctor, then turned her attention back to Lydia. "He was a mistake, Ms. Page. He should never have been allowed in the program. I swear to god I'm going to find out who did this and—"

"What?" Lydia asked, her heart starting to pound hard once again. What was happening? What had she done by trusting these people? "What the hell is going on?"

"He isn't human, Ms. Page."

It was as if the lawyer switch suddenly flicked on and Lydia moved closer to the woman. "Really? That's how you're going to play this? Telling me I have an alien baby? Not only is that pathetic and ridiculous, but it makes you—"

"You have heard about the race of shape shifters discovered out in the bayous?" the doctor asked.

A thread of unease moved through her. "Yes, of course. I've seen them on TV and online. The Pantera, I think they're called. But what does that have to do with—" She whipped around to face Erin.

For the first time since Lydia had seen the woman, she genuinely looked distressed. "I don't know how this happened, Ms. Page. But I swear to you we will find out."

Flies were buzzing in her head. She couldn't hear very well. Her skin felt prickly too. And she was shaking her head. "No."

"I'm very sorry."

She started to back up. "That's impossible."

"Your blood tests confirm the match," Erin said.

Reeling, Lydia turned away and headed for the door. She had her fingers around the knob when Erin called out to her.

"Take the day. We'll schedule the termination tomorrow morning."

Tears pricked Lydia's eyes.

"You'll only need to wait a few weeks and we can try again—"

Her hand left the door and went to her belly. "No. Never." She whirled around. "This baby is mine."

Erin and the doctor both stared at her like she was insane. And maybe she was.

"Ms. Page," the doctor began. "Besides this being against our laws of nature, the Pantera will not look kindly on this mistake. Our government is working with theirs to foster a relationship. It's only at the beginning stages. We don't know how these...beasts...will react."

Beasts? It was as if the man had sent a knife through her heart. She didn't know what was coming. Didn't know how she was going to manage any of it. But she did know that she was going to protect this child from people like these.

"You could be in danger if anyone found out." Erin had her arms crossed over her chest. She looked pensive. "Not everyone has sympathy and understanding for these animals—this new species."

"Like you?" Lydia asked bitingly.

Erin's lips thinned. "I urge you to think very carefully about this, Ms. Page. And we hope to see you back here in the morning."

"I don't have to think about anything," Lydia told her fiercely, her hand finding the doorknob once again. "No one is taking this baby from me. Pantera, human—it belongs to me."

As she swung the door wide and walked out of the doctor's office, she felt both sets of eyes on her back.

CHAPTER 3

His cat had taken him to the edge of the Wildlands, but after his shift into his male form, his mind and body, and something he couldn't explain—or resist—had led him into New Orleans. He'd been there a hundred times for both business and pleasure, but this was the first time he'd had no clear purpose.

As he roamed the sunlit streets, enjoying a respite from the many hours of sick stomach and fuzzy head, he wondered why he was drawn here—what his cat was after.

Who it was after.

It wasn't unusual for a Pantera to follow a feeling, an instinct—see where it led. But it was an unusual practice for Roch. He rarely used his instincts unless he was in his puma form. In his male form, as a Suit, he relied on information, deduction and logic.

Bracketed by a small crowd of people, Roch noticed a woman walking toward him. She was beautiful, with long red hair and green eyes—eyes that moved over him with interest.

"Hi there," she called out.

It was the strangest thing. Roch wasn't the kind of male who pursued a woman, hard and relentless, but he did show his interest with a few words and a smile. Today, however, he had neither. Nothing. No interest at all.

Well, not in the redhead, anyway.

Just as she passed him with an irritated eye roll, he felt a surge of heat so powerful and electric, he turned toward it, like a flower into the sun. Or a Pantera male into a storefront. He glanced up at the sign before him. *Break For Beignets*. What the hell was this, a diner? A donut shop? And why was he being drawn here?

With heat still blazing inside him, he opened the door and went in. He was immediately met with an overpoweringly sweet scent and a long line of customers. Clearly, everyone wanted a beignet this morning. Everyone but Roch. He wasn't hungry. In fact, despite the wondrous heat radiating from his chest, he was starting to feel sick again. *Goddamit. What the fuck is going on?*

He scanned the line, looking for something, anything that would stand out to him. When that turned up nothing, his eyes cut left, moved over the six tables and the people sitting at them. Lovers, businesspeople, family—

His gut screamed, then felt as if it had been split in half by a dull ax. He blinked to clear his vision, which was flickering black and white. Seated at the smallest table near the back was a woman he didn't know. Didn't recognize. And yet he did.

His breath seized inside his lungs and for a second, he just stared at her. Maybe twenty-seven or twenty-eight, and human, she was the most beautiful woman he'd ever seen in his life. She had delicate features that called to him to touch. But a strong presence that made him wary. The sunlight streaming in from the window at her right made her masses of tight blond curls glow like a halo, and when she glanced up from her coffee and caught his gaze, he saw that her eyes were an extraordinary shade of violet. Christ. Who was this woman? And why had he been drawn here to her? Because, hell, he knew she was the reason he'd come to New Orleans today.

He started her way, his gaze taking in her form-fitting gray suit. She was tall, with small, firm breasts, and long, lean legs that could wrap a male's waist and hold on tight while he—

He shut his thoughts down before they managed to take root. Take root and multiply.

He stopped when he reached her table, and found himself tongue-tied. Unheard of. What was going on? Why was he so attracted to her, by her? No. No... Attracted was too gentle a word for what he felt when he looked at this woman. Possessed was better. More accurate.

"You can take the chair."

She was speaking to him; a clear, sensual sound from lips so naturally full and pink they made his mouth water. *Shit*. And she was looking at him with those large, expressive, violet eyes rimmed with extraordinarily long lashes.

"Excuse me?" Roch said, trying to reason what he was doing, and why.

"You want that, right?" She pointed to the black iron chair across from her. "Feel free. I know it's crazy busy in here."

He glanced around, then came back to her. "The tables are all full." He sounded like a fool, an insane male. And yet he couldn't stop himself.

"I suppose you can sit here," she said, though her tone was cautious. "But I have to warn you, I'm not going to be great company. It's been a shitastic morning."

Tell me, his cat purred from inside his chest. Tell me what's wrong and I'll fix it. Whatever it is.

Ignoring the overzealous feline inside of him, Roch pulled out the chair and sat down. "I'm sorry about your morning. Nothing like a donut to make things right, though."

She smiled and the gesture seemed to light up her entire face. He stared at her. Hard. He couldn't help himself. Besides her beauty, she made him feel...right somehow. It was like walking in the front door of his house and sitting down on the couch. He felt comfortable and warm. And drawn. So fucking drawn.

"Have you ordered yet?" she asked, her eyes flickering with humor. "Maybe you need a donut too."

"Maybe." A smile tugged at his lips. "But alas, the line..."

She glanced past him and nodded. "Well, I'm not very hungry." She pushed her plate toward him. "You can have mine."

Roch's eyes settled on the pastry, then lifted to regard her. "Have we met?" he asked. "I feel as if I know you."

She laughed softly. "I want to say that's a pretty tired pick-up line. But," she stopped and shook her head, "I think we may have." Her brows drew together. "Are you an attorney? Or do you have a job in the legal profession?"

"No." Was she an attorney? He knew nothing about her. And yet he truly felt as though he knew everything.

"Maybe college?" she suggested. "Where did you go to school?"

"I didn't." His nostrils flared. She smelled like heaven. Flowers and some kind of spice. "Have you been to The Cougar's Den in La Pierre? Or out near the bayous?"

"No." She laughed. "You know what it probably is? I look like someone you know and vice versa."

No. No. "I don't think it's that simple," he said, his chest flickering with tension.

"I think it has to be. Or maybe online, Facebook or—"

He couldn't stand it any longer. He leaned in and whispered, "Are you connected with the Pantera somehow?"

Her eyes widened and her lips parted. "What did you just say?"

His jaw tight, he glanced around, then turned back to her. "Do you know of the Pantera?"

Her face went as white as the powdered sugar on top of her beignet. "Oh my god," she said on a gasp. "Oh my god. Those assholes." Her eyes narrowed on him. "Freaking Haymore works fast."

Haymore? Roch stared at her in confusion. Who the hell was Haymore? His gut rippled with tension. Was this her male?

"Listen up, dickhead," she ground out, trying to keep her voice low as she stared him down. "No matter what you've been sent here to do or to offer me, I will never end this pregnancy."

Roch's guts screamed with heat and sickness. Those violet eyes had turned fierce and protective. Pregnancy? She was pregnant? What the hell? Bile claimed his throat and he wished for his cat to take over so he didn't puke all over the untouched beignet.

"I'm leaving now," the woman said tightly. "Follow me and I'm going straight to the police." She leaned toward him then and whispered, "Leave me alone and you'll never hear from me again. No one will ever know this child is half Pantera."

Roch's body started to vibrate as the woman grabbed her purse and stood up. He reached for her, took her wrist, his eyes piercing into hers. "You are carrying a Pantera young?" he hissed, careful to keep his voice low. No doubt they were already attracting attention.

It wasn't possible. She couldn't be... With the curse... He froze. The curse had lifted only weeks ago. But, Christ, if it was true, who had planted their seed inside of her?

Feral anger rippled through him.

Which Pantera male had lain with this woman? Touched her? Ran their hands through those soft, blond curls while they—

She yanked her arm away, cutting off questions he had no right to be asking. "Fine. Play stupid." She seemed tough, hard, pissed off, but the fear was bright in her eyes. "Just don't bother me ever again."

Bother her? That's not what he wanted. "You're putting yourself in danger," he managed to grind out. "By being here. By being out—" He was about to say out of the bayou, but she stopped him with a hard stare.

"I don't care." She glanced around at the nearby tables, then turned back to him and whispered, "I will do anything to protect my child."

"Even if that child is part animal?" he asked, amazed.

"Fuck you," she ground out.

Stunned, every muscle in his body tense and ready to spring, his guts clenching with every breath he expelled, Roch watched as the woman left the table and hurried out of the shop.

A bag of Chinese take-out in one hand and a

book on what to expect during pregnancy in the other, Lydia thanked her doorman and headed for the elevator. After the morning she'd had she just wanted to hide out in her condo this afternoon. Take a bath, and binge-watch Orange Is the New Black while stuffing her face with cream cheese wontons.

Once inside, she hit the button for the third floor and leaned back against the metal wall. She was trying to assure herself that the people at The Haymore Center would leave her alone now that she'd threatened going to the police, outing their mistake, but she couldn't help feeling afraid. Not for herself, oddly, but for the little life growing inside her. If this baby was truly half Pantera, how was she going to protect him or her? Especially if there were people out there who looked at her child and saw an animal?

The elevator door opened and she stepped out, headed down the hall. Was it possible to keep it a secret? Or would her half human child end up being able to shift into a cat one day in the middle of Show and Tell?

Okay, tomorrow, she mused, nearly dropping her book as she tried to free a hand to get her keys. She'd think about this tomorrow.

"Let me help you?" came a male voice a few feet away.

Lydia's head lifted and her heart nearly dropped onto the carpet under her feet. She froze, her keys instantly forgotten. Clutching the food and the book to her chest, she took in the man standing just outside her door. It was him. Of course it was him. The guy from the beignet place. Her insides pinched. From fear, and lord, from something else entirely. Something she refused to name. Something she should not be feeling at all.

Her gaze tracked over him. He was terrifyingly good-looking. Tall, lean, big hands, thick wrists, dark blond hair and icy blue eyes that warned of a highly intelligent mind. Just like earlier, he wore a black suit, white shirt, and dark purple tie, and as he walked toward her it was like witnessing the very essence of confidence, sexuality and ultra masculinity.

"This is disturbing," she said, trying like hell to remain cool and calm, and act like she could kick his ass if she had to. "You outside my door." Dammit. Her voice was shaking. Or maybe that was her insides. It was just...the way he was looking at her. Not like he wanted to do her harm, but like he wanted to know what her skin tasted like.

She blushed and walked past him to her door.

"I'm sorry," he said. "I'm not trying to scare you."

She could feel him behind her. His warmth. "Too late." She transferred the book and food bag to her left arm, then went searching—not for her keys this time, but her cellphone. If this gorgeous bastard from Haymore tried anything, she was calling the police.

"I just need to know," he said, coming around her and leaning all six feet, suit-clad, hard jawed gorgeousness against the doorframe. "Are you certain you're carrying a Pantera child?"

The need to drop everything and cover her belly with her hands, protect her tiny child, was intensely strong. But Lydia kept her composure. "That's an odd question for the man who's representing the very company whose samples I used."

"I'm not representing this Haymore you speak of."

She turned to look at him just as her hand closed around her cell.

His eyes darkened to a stormy sky blue. "And I'm not a man."

Heat and panic erupted within her. Her breathing shallow and uneven, she brought her cellphone out of her purse and quickly dialed 911. "You need to get the hell out of here. Maybe get yourself to a psych ward. The cops are coming."

But the cellphone never made it to her ear. The man slipped it from her so fast she hardly felt it leave her hand. He stabbed the off button, then turned to look at her.

"You need to come with me, Ms. Page."

Her heart was beating so fast, she worried she might pass out. "And you need to run before I scream my head off."

"I am not going to hurt you," he insisted tightly. In fact, he looked put out, insulted by her suggestion. "I am Pantera, and I want to help you."

The book she was carrying slipped from her

arms and dropped onto the floor. Her mind whirred. And she tried to keep up with her thoughts—with what he'd just said to her. *Pantera*. This tall, imposing, stunning, gorgeous nut case was Pantera?

No.

She stared into his eyes. She didn't believe him. Couldn't. But then she saw something flash within those ice blue orbs. Something she couldn't explain, but something her body, skin, and blood recognized.

She gasped, covered her mouth. "It's not possible."

"What samples are you talking about?" he asked. "What did you get from this Haymore Center?"

Oh god. Was this really happening? "I was artificially inseminated." She couldn't believe she was saying this, telling him this.

Something flickered in his blue eyes. Gratification? Or relief? "So you have not lain with one of our males, then? No Pantera has a claim on you?"

Lydia stared at him. "No." The way he spoke. The words he used. Could this be real? Could he actually be a Pantera shifter?

"If the child is Pantera," the man continued as if what they were discussing was not completely insane-sounding, "wouldn't you want to know its origins, community, history and medical issues?"

"I don't want to do this," she said, digging into her purse, grabbing her keys. "Just go.

Please. I don't know how you found me or who you really are, but—"

He sniffed with irritation. "Unless you're thinking of hiding the child? Is that it? Hiding it away so the humans don't have to see it." The sudden ferocity in his eyes was a living, breathing thing. "Perhaps you're ashamed of its—"

"Hey!" His words, and his accusation, were like boiling water on a hot day. Forgetting her fear, she whirled on him and air-stabbed him with her key. "Never," she said through gritted teeth. "Okay? I would never be ashamed of my child."

She turned back and jammed her key into the lock. This was madness. All of this. She needed time. She needed to think. Maybe he would go away. Maybe he'd leave a number where she could reach him. Dammit! She was so confused. She pushed the door open.

"Come with me, Lydia," he said.

Just as she stepped inside her hallway, her head came around. "You know my name."

He nodded, as if that was answer enough.

Apprehension tugged at her insides. "If I say no, you'll try and take me anyway, won't you?"

Sharp eyebrows lifted over intense blue eyes. "Are you saying no?"

Her breathing uneven, she slipped farther inside. She was just about to shut the door in his face and on those words, when she heard a noise coming from her living room. Her heart slammed against her ribs as true fear coursed through her.

The man's lip curled and his nostrils flared. "Don't move."

Without another word, he rushed past her— so fast she barely saw him. Lydia stood there frozen, trying to decide what to do. Suddenly, the sounds of fists hitting bone, and glass breaking against hardwood rent the air. Fuck! Where was her cell? Did he have it? Could she get into the kitchen and use the house phone?

But before she could make any kind of move, the man emerged from the shadows of her living room. Calm, cool, looking as though he hadn't been touched.

"Leave the food," he said tightly, his eyes moving over her, examining every inch of her. "I'll feed you once we get to the Wildlands."

Lydia noticed she'd dropped the bag of Chinese on the floor. The book, however, was still clutched to her chest.

"What was that?" she demanded in a thin whisper.

He took her hand in his. It was cool and large and callused. "Come on. It's not safe here. That bastard had a gun."

CHAPTER 4

"Roch," he told her as she hesitated in the backseat of the cab they'd taken from New Orleans to La Pierre.

It wasn't his usual method of travel. He liked to run, or, when he was traveling for business, use one of the vehicles from the Pantera's car club. But he was in a hurry today, and he wouldn't have Lydia walking any farther than necessary.

She glanced up at him, her expression wary, yet intrigued. A look Roch was getting used to with her.

"That's your name?" she asked. "Roch?"

He nodded as the cab pulled to a stop in front of The Cougar's Den. He quickly paid the driver, then opened the door and stepped out. He offered Lydia a hand. "Come. We need to walk a little now."

She took it, and Roch tried not to purr at the feeling of her soft skin against his palm. If it was possible, she looked even more beautiful in the rich, afternoon light of the bayou. Her curls were pulled back off her flawless face in a loose ponytail, and the warmth of the day was making her cheeks flush pink.

He led her out of The Cougar's Den parking lot and toward the bayou and the Wildlands, making sure their route through the terrain was relatively uncomplicated. It had been nearly impossible to keep his eyes off of her on their drive. His hands, too. He'd felt her anxiety and had wanted to comfort her. But he needed to remember that she didn't belong to him. He was merely discovery, protection and delivery. If she truly was carrying a Pantera cub within her, priority number one was going to be to find out how that had happened. How a clinic in New Orleans had managed to get their hands on Pantera sperm samples.

Then they were going to have to find the father.

As they walked, heat and irritation slashed through him at the thought. Not to mention the words, and the warning: *I found her and I get to keep her.*

Foolish male, he chided himself.

"Just for the record," she said as they trudged through thick grasses and around massive cypresses. "I'm coming with you because I decided to."

"Of course."

"Not because someone forced me," she continued, her tone no doubt similar to the one she used in a court of law. "I don't do anything I don't want to do."

"I believe that," he said with a hint of

amusement. He would like to see her in court, badgering witnesses, fighting for justice for her client. He imagined she'd be magnificent.

"Are you making fun of me?" she asked with just a touch of humor.

"Not at all," he said. "There is no denying that you're a strong-willed female. Much like our Pantera females."

"Really?"

"Yes. You'll fit in well."

"I'm not planning on fitting in, Roch."

Christ, his name on her lips was like a stroke to his skin with a goddamn feather. As they walked through the lush flora and the sun grazed his skin, he couldn't help but imagine her saying it again...in his ear...on his neck.

Against his mouth.

He growled softly and forced those thoughts and images back. Hell, he should kick them the hell out. Never to return again. He had no right to them. Dangerous. Impossible.

When the border of the Wildlands finally came into view he heaved a sigh of relief. She would be someone else's responsibility soon. He'd get her to Medical and under Dr. Julia's care. Parish's mate was human too, and she would serve this purpose well. Then he'd find out who the father of Lydia's cub was—and how this Haymore Center had gotten a hold of Pantera samples.

His stomach rolled suddenly and he groaned. *Shit*. What was going on with him? He stopped and took a breath, wondering if he was going to actually get sick in front of his new guest. That would be great. Really fucking fantastic.

Lydia moved closer and put her hand on his shoulder. "You okay?"

He sucked in air. Not because of his wrecked stomach, but because of her touch. It made his skin and chest tighten, and, Goddess help him, his cock twitch.

"What's wrong?" she asked, sounding surprisingly concerned. "Can I do something?"

"No. It's nothing. Just haven't been feeling well lately." When she eased her hand back and stepped away from him, he laughed. "Don't worry, Lydia. It's not catching. Something I ate or drank." Or who the hell knew?

"Sorry," she said with a soft laugh.

"No problem."

"I just want to protect the baby."

"As do I."

She stilled, her eyes finding his. They were the color of a Dyesse lily, and the warmth they gave off made him ache with a hunger he'd never known before. Shit, what was he going to do about this? This attraction. No, this...*crush* he seemed to have on a human female—a human female who was carrying a Pantera male's cub?

Maybe the male wouldn't want it.

Maybe the male wouldn't want her.

It was his cat. The puma's thoughts, not his own.

A deep growl erupted from his throat.

"Roch?" she said, sounding worried.

"It's okay," he said quickly, diffusing her concern. "We're just on the border of the Wildlands."

As they entered a thick cluster of trees, and the scent of the bayou wafted over them, Lydia stopped and looked around. The sun filtering through the treetops, changing the colors of the leaves from sunny yellow and green to pale orange. "Wow. It's beautiful here."

Roch felt a swell of pride at her words. It was good she could see what he saw. Good for her cub, if it was indeed Pantera. "You haven't seen anything yet," he said.

Her eyes met his and they were warm and excited, and Roch had to stop himself from reaching out and brushing her cheek with his fingertips.

"Well, let's go then," she said, starting off toward another massive cypress.

"Not on foot," Roch called out to her.

She turned, her brows knit together. "Then how?"

"Don't be afraid, all right?"

"Afraid of what?" she asked.

He took a deep breath, trying to calm his cat. He could feel it pacing inside of him, wanting to get out. Wanting to meet her. In a flash of movement, he shifted into his puma. The cat snarled and stretched, and instantly, Roch felt healthy and strong.

He turned and growled softly at Lydia. She was standing there staring at him, her eyes wide, her mouth open. But surprisingly, she didn't look scared. Just awestruck.

"Oh my god." She shook her head. "I know this is real, but it just feels...it looks...you are so beautiful..."

Roch's cat purred with pleasure, then gestured to its back with its enormous head.

She looked from his face to his back. "You want me to ride on you?" she asked, her voice reed-thin.

He stalked toward her, growling at her again. When he pressed his massive body against her side, she nearly toppled over.

"I guess that's a yes," she said with a reluctant laugh. She climbed onto his back, her sweet weight pressing into his muscles, then leaned over so her lips were near his cat's ear.

The puma nearly lost its mind. It lifted its head and howled into the fragrant bayou.

"I hope I'm not too heavy," she whispered, wrapping her arms around its neck.

A sound almost like laughter erupted from Roch's cat before it took off into the trees.

Lydia studied the pretty young woman with the pale skin and long black hair who had come into her room at the Medical facility just moments ago. Her name was Ashe, and she seemed nice. Hell, everyone Lydia had encountered so far seemed nice. She wasn't sure what she'd expected. After reading an article about them in one of the more reputable newspapers, maybe she'd imagined a more domineering species. But she hadn't encountered that yet. Unless she counted Roch. He definitely had a bit of the domineering side. But everyone else had been very welcoming, almost gentle. No doubt they wanted her to feel comfortable as they all figured this out together.

She felt so unsure about being here, yet so curious too. Riding on Roch's back, her arms around his warm, powerful neck, had been one of the most incredible experiences of her life. And seeing the Wildlands up close, its obvious beauty and quiet magic made her ache to see more, see everything. If her child was really a part of all this, a Pantera, then she wanted to explore, find out as much as she could about them and their way of life.

"I know you must have a million questions," Ashe said, coming over to the bed and sitting down. "And I'm sure Doctor Julia answered some of them when she took blood samples and your medical history earlier. But I can offer you something that no one else can." The woman's brown eyes flashed with companionable mystery.

"What's that?" Lydia asked, curious.

"I'm human," she said. "And my mate is Pantera. We have a new baby."

Lydia didn't say anything for a moment. She was kind of shocked. None of that was mentioned in the article she'd read. She had no idea that Pantera and humans were interacting. And mating? Was that like marrying?

"You're human?" she repeated.

Ashe nodded. "And let me just tell you, when I first came here and saw all of this, I was shocked and scared, and I didn't know what to do. I'd met my mate outside of the Wildlands without knowing he was Pantera."

"Oh wow," Lydia said. How had that happened? Maybe Ashe would share the story with her sometime, if she felt comfortable.

"Right?" Ashe grinned, reached over and placed her hand on Lydia's. "But after the shock wore off, I swear to you, I never knew such happiness existed. Being here, with Raphael and my baby, it's the best thing that has ever happened to me."

A soft smile touched Lydia's mouth. "It sounds wonderful. But you knew your mate, right? You wanted to be with him?"

Ashe nodded.

"That's not how this went down for me," Lydia said. "I didn't want a relationship. I'd done that and gotten hurt. Really hurt."

Ashe gave her a sympathetic look and squeezed her hand.

"I only wanted a child." Lydia touched her stomach with her free hand. "So being here in the Wildlands, it's not about romance and building a relationship with the father. I don't even know who it is. I'm nervous to find out, you know?"

"Of course. And no one is going to push you to have a paternity test. That'll be your choice. And when you're ready, *if* you're ready, all you have to do is let Doctor Julia know."

"I suppose the first thing is to find out if my baby is truly part Pantera." Lydia laughed softly. "The donor I used was supposed to be anonymous and...human."

"I understand," Ashe said. "I really do." She took a deep breath. "Listen, you're going to be around for a few days, right?"

Lydia nodded. She had agreed to that. She wanted that. Truly. She wanted to find out the truth about the baby's biological history. And if the child was half Pantera, she needed to learn as much as she could about them, so someday she could tell her child where they came from. It was amazing really, Lydia thought. Back in New Orleans, every human she'd come in contact with had wanted her to terminate her pregnancy ASAP. But here in the Wildlands it had been the complete opposite—they'd been almost reverent about the pregnancy, and her. She understood why Ashe felt so happy and content.

"You can, of course, stay here at Medical," Ashe began. "It's cozy." She shrugged. "In a clinical, Nurturers-gawking-at-you kind of way."

Lydia laughed. Nurturers seemed to be the medical staff here. The caretakers and scientists. Her eyes drifted to the door. She wondered if Roch was a Nurturer. She didn't think so. He didn't seem particularly nurturing. Protective, strong-willed, handsome, sexy, maybe. But not nurturing.

She swallowed hard and felt relieved when Ashe continued talking.

"I'd love it if you'd come stay with us."

Lydia turned to gape at the woman. "Us?"

"Me and my mate, Raphael. And our daughter, Soyala, of course." Ashe stood up. She looked very trendy. Human, come to think of it, in her black peasant top, skinny jeans and boots. "Now, I have to warn you, she's only a few weeks old, so you might be woken up at all hours of the night. But it's homey there and if you needed anything...well...to talk or whatever—"

The pull to say yes was a strong one. She liked this woman. A lot. And to remain in her soft, supportive light sounded so appealing. But the last thing she wanted was to impose on anyone. Especially a new family.

"I'll stay here," Lydia said quickly and gently.

Ashe looked instantly bummed. "It's the baby thing, right? I swear no one wants to hang out with us anymore. All the poopy diapers and breastfeeding."

Lydia laughed again. "No. God, no. Not at all. In fact, the baby thing is a huge plus for me. It's just—"

"What?"

"I don't want to impose."

Ashe made a shocked sound deep in her throat. "Okay, that's silly and crazy. You're staying with us. Period. End of story. I made lasagna for dinner tonight, and garlic bread. Who in their right mind can turn down garlic bread?"

It was virtually impossible to not like this woman. Lydia shrugged. "I do love me some garlic bread."

Ashe beamed, clasped her hands together. "Perfect. As soon as you're done here, I'll take you home. We're pretty much the same size and you can borrow anything you like." She glanced at her watch. "It shouldn't be more than a half hour, I think. Raphael, Baptiste and Roch are having a powwow out in the hall somewhere."

"They are?" Lydia felt her cheeks warm. She'd wondered where the man—the male, she'd have to get used to that—had gone off to. She wanted so much to get to know him. This man who had found her in *Break for Beignets,* saved her from whatever had been in her apartment, then brought her here. She wanted to know how he'd done that. And why?

"So, this Roch who found me," Lydia began, trying her damnedest to sound casual. "Who is he?"

"He works with my mate. They're what's called Diplomatic Faction. Or 'Suits.' They're like politicians or facilitators in our world."

Suit. Diplomat. Well, that certainly fit. And made him sound even more attractive than he already was. She cleared her throat. "Does he have a mate?"

"Roch?" Ashe started laughing. "Oh, no. He's a total loner. Really enjoys the single life, if you know what I mean."

Lydia did. Dammit.

"Totally unattached by choice," Ashe added. "But a good guy. Loyal, and deeply dedicated to his work. Even more so than

Raphael, I think—which is saying something."

A loner, and a workaholic. Kind of like her. "So, no family dinners," she said with a forced smile.

"No. Not unless he's invited to one." Ashe paused, then her eyes narrowed playfully and studied Lydia. "Wait a sec. I could invite him?"

Lydia's heart seized inside her chest. "No, no, that's fine."

The woman smiled broadly. "I have more than enough lasagna."

"I was just curious," Lydia explained, hoping her cheeks weren't too pink. "He was the one who found me and brought me here. I wanted to thank him or...something." God, she sounded like a moron.

"It is pretty extraordinary how that all happened," Ashe remarked thoughtfully. "Actually, it's unheard of. Everyone's talking about it."

Lydia didn't understand. "What do you mean?"

"A male Pantera finding a pregnant human female." Her brows lifted. "Especially one he's never met. Or slept with." She nodded. "Extraordinary. And something I'm sure Raphael and the others are trying to figure out as we speak."

CHAPTER 5

Roch paced the small patch of moonlit grass behind Medical. Due to his erratic and overassertive behavior when he'd brought Lydia in, Raphael, Dr. Julia and Jean-Baptiste had all thought it best that any discussion involving the human woman be done outside the building.

At first, Roch had blown them off, didn't believe that he was acting in any way but professionally when it came to her welfare and situation. But then he caught himself sniffing at her door, even growling at any Nurturers who tried to enter.

He'd gone willingly with them at that point.

"We have both Hunters and Suits dispatched to this Haymore Center," Raphael said, his tone just a decibel above a growl. "We'll find out exactly who they are and what happened. And how a mistake like this could occur. If indeed, impregnating a human woman with Pantera DNA was a mistake."

"It has to be a mistake," Doc Julia uttered, more to herself than to Raphael.

Jean-Baptiste inhaled deeply. "So, the blood samples show—"

"Yes," she said, her tone a strange combination of excitement and concern. "The baby is both human and Pantera." She lifted her gaze first to meet Raphael's, then Baptiste's. "Do you know what this means?"

Jean-Baptiste lifted his pierced eyebrow. "We need to find the father?"

Roch's lip curled with irritation, but he kept on pacing. Down the path aways he spotted Chayton, the man who had been taken over by Shakpi not long ago. He was working with a Nurturer and the Shaman-in-training, Sage, Lian's new mate, on some kind of trust exercise.

Poor bastard, he mused. Forget trust. It was going to be a miracle if the man actually managed to have some semblance of a normal life.

"Yes, we'll need to find the father," Julia put in. "When Lydia is ready to allow the testing. But it also means that with Shakpi gone, the curse has truly lifted. We could be seeing pregnancies throughout the Wildlands now."

Everyone was silent for a moment, letting that information seep in.

"My Genny," Jean-Baptiste uttered almost reverently. "She has wanted a cub so badly."

"This could be a new beginning," Raphael agreed. "But before we start the celebration, we must know how this human pregnancy occurred. Roch?"

Roch stopped pacing and turned to look at the three Pantera, who were all staring intently at him now. "What?"

"Are you certain you don't know her?"

"Am I certain?" He cursed. "Do you really think I'm the kind of male who wouldn't remember someone I bedded four weeks ago? That I'm that low, that vile?"

Raphael didn't answer. Just kept his gaze locked on the male. Whatever his personal opinion, he wanted an answer.

"Christ, no," Roch answered tersely. "All right? I've never seen her before in my life."

I would remember. Hell, I'd never be able to forget. Never be able to look at another female again after her.

"It seems improbable," Baptiste put in.

Roch whirled on the heavily tattooed Nurturer and flashed him a feral glare.

Baptiste chuckled and put his palms up in surrender. One had the name of his mate, Genevieve, inked onto it. "Easy, brother. My point is only that you went searching for her—"

"I went to New Orleans. There was no search."

"And you found her, brought her back here. And look at you now."

"What?" Roch ground out. "Look at what?"

"You're acting mated," Jean-Baptiste said calmly. "You're acting like me and Raphael and Parish when someone gets too close or threatens our females."

Raphael nodded in agreement. "I have to say it's true. I've never seen you like this, Roch."

"I've been ill, that's all," he tossed out.

"Don't think so."

Confusion, irritation and anger all rose up to claim him. "What the hell are you implying, Raphael?"

But it wasn't Raphael who answered.

"That this child could be yours," Doc Julia put in, her expression amazed.

A knot formed in Roch's chest. He ripped his gaze from them and stalked away. Just a few feet. Then he stopped and turned around. "Impossible," he hissed at them.

"Is it?" Raphael said.

"I've never seen her before." Roch looked up to the heavens. "I swear on Opela. And even if I had, I don't take risks like that. Even when we were cursed, I made sure the females beneath me were protected."

"Beneath him," Baptiste uttered under his breath.

"Beneath me, on top of me—"

"All right. Too much information, brother," Raphael said.

Roch snarled at them. "You can all go to hell."

"Hey," Julia put in, her eyes bright with amusement. "I didn't go there. I wanted to. But I didn't."

"Oh fuck," Baptiste said, his tone instantly grave.

"What?" Raphael said. "What's wrong?"

"Remember back when we found out

about the curse? We all had samples taken from us for the purpose of testing. Blood, urine, semen..."

Something curled inside of Roch's belly.

"*Oh fuck*, is right," Raphael said, his mind working behind his green eyes. "That was over fifty years ago. I had forgotten."

"Would someone have given those samples to a human lab?" Julia asked, the moon above casting an eerie glow to her skin.

"It's possible, I suppose. We were trying in any way we could to keep our race going. But it would've been covert, against our laws. The experiments were only to be done in our laboratory."

Jean-Baptiste looked murderous. No doubt deducing that whoever had leaked samples was probably a Nurturer. "We need to find out who did this."

"Maybe Hiss will know?" Roch put in.

"I will take that bastard out with my bare hands if he's in any way responsible," Raphael threatened. Then he took a deep breath and cursed. "If this is true, we're in deep shit." His nostrils flared. "We can shut down The Haymore Center and recover the remaining samples, but who knows how many human women have been inseminated already."

"We could have males running off, going in search of their offspring," Baptiste put in. "All we can hope for is what Roch did. Find the mother of the cub and bring her back here."

"The child is not mine!" Roch roared.

All three of them went silent and turned to look at him.

"Most males would be pleased to know they had sired a Pantera cub," Jean-Baptiste said, his chin lifting a fraction.

"Not this way!" Roch returned, his chest tightening around his heart muscle. "Christ. Not this way." He cursed and uttered a battered, "Not in a lab."

"You have feelings for this woman," Julia said, her eyes going wide.

Roch didn't answer her. In fact, he didn't acknowledge any of them. He was done. Fractured by the possibility they'd just laid out before him. The impossible, amazing, horrifying possibility.

Turning away, he headed down the path, shifting into his puma state just before he was lost in the shadows of the garden.

Twenty-four hours ago Lydia had been in her apartment, standing at the kitchen counter, eating a supermarket salad and wondering what the following day would bring. Who knew it would bring so much: a firing, a possible Pantera baby, kindness, danger, beauty, confusion and—she glanced around the table at the small family gathered there—an altogether different existence.

Truly, she didn't know what was going to happen from this day onward, but here in the Wildlands she felt no fear about herself or her child's future. Maybe that was naive. Or maybe she had an example of what was possible right in front of her. Standing over the long, rustic wood table in her lovely two-story antebellum home, sliding a ginormous piece of lasagna onto Lydia's plate.

She started to laugh.

Ashe glanced up. "What? Does it look bad? Too runny?"

"It looks amazing," Lydia assured her.

"I swear I didn't go crazy with the sauce."

"*Ma chérie*," Raphael put in, his gold-green eyes warm with love as he ran his hand over her hip. "I think she's just worried she can't eat it all."

"Oh," Ashe laughed, her cheeks flushing pink. "Well, no worries about that. Just do what you can." She gave Lydia a knowing smile. "But there is the growing baby to think of."

"Cub," Raphael corrected, then gave Lydia a gentle smile. "It's not too early to get used to that."

"Or how much the little fur ball likes to eat," Ashe said, glancing down at her beautiful blond baby, who was fast asleep in her raised bassinet beside the table. "Even when they're inside you."

"I'll remember that," Lydia said with a grin.

Ashe sighed as she sat down and picked up her fork. "We're so excited for you, Lydia. All the Pantera are. It's such a blessing, and we just want to make sure you have everything you need. We want you and the cub healthy."

"Yes, we do," came a male voice behind her.

A ripple of heat moved through Lydia's body as she turned and caught sight of Roch standing in the archway between the grand entryway and the dining room. Gone was the suit and tie. And in their place were black jogging pants and a black t-shirt. Both molded to his incredible body. He looked sporty and masculine and hot, and she tried not to drool as she stared at him.

"How did you get in here?" Raphael asked good-naturedly.

"Door was open."

"And you didn't think to knock?"

He walked over to the table and pulled out the chair beside Lydia. "I was invited to dinner."

"By whom?" Raphael demanded.

Ashe cleared her throat as both her mate and Lydia turned to look at her. She cut another sizable piece of lasagna and slid it onto an empty plate. "He hasn't been feeling very well, so I thought a little home cooking..."

"Poor little cub," Raphael said with heavy sarcasm, turning to his colleague and friend and giving him an amused grin.

Roch tossed the male a fierce glare.

"Are you going upstairs afterward and having Ashe tuck you into bed? Read you a story?" He paused, realizing what he'd just suggested. He rounded on his mate. "No, *ma chère*. Please don't do that."

"Not a chance," she answered. "Only one who's getting tucked in tonight is you."

He growled softly at her. "Mmm, I like that."

"Hey," Roch said, standing up. "I can go."

"No," Lydia said without thinking.

He turned to look at her, and the heat and hunger in his gaze was blinding. In fact, it made her heart race like a rabbit's. He liked her. She was sure of it.

"Sit down," Raphael called out to him. "I was just giving you a hard time. Let my mate serve you a piece of lasagna the size of your head. It would make her so happy."

"Hey!" Ashe said, then started laughing.

"Don't get upset, *ma chérie*. You know I live to make you happy."

"And you always do." She blushed, and he leaned in and kissed her deeply and hungrily until she sighed.

Roch turned to Lydia. "How are you?"

"Good. Fine." Glad to see you. You look gorgeous. Then again, you always look—

"Are you happy staying here?" he asked, his expression raw with concern. "You don't have to. I'm sure you won't get any sleep with the cub."

"We've already discussed that, Roch," Ashe remarked after coming up for air.

He turned to his plate and picked up his fork. "She needs more than food to keep her healthy and well. She needs sleep."

"Well, she wouldn't get that at Medical," Ashe replied, offering him some bread.

"There are other options."

"Like what? Your place?"

Lydia's heart sprang into her throat. She didn't want to hear his answer to that. Yes or no. Either option concerned her. "I'm happy here," she stated quickly, resolutely. "And I love being around that cutie-pie over there."

Roch glanced at the sleeping baby. "She's getting big."

Ashe nearly melted with motherly happiness. "She is."

"And she looks like you, Ashe. Which is lucky for her."

Raphael glanced up from his nearly consumed lasagna and gave his friend a good-natured growl.

Popping a piece of garlic bread in her mouth, Ashe turned to Lydia. "So, is your family from New Orleans?"

"They are. Were. They're gone now. My mom passed away a few months back."

Ashe's expression fell into a lovely mask of empathy. "I'm sorry."

"Thank you." She touched her belly, which now sported just the very beginnings of a rise. "I'm excited for new family to come into my life."

Ashe nodded. "Of course you are."

"What do you do for work, Lydia?" Raphael asked her.

"I'm a lawyer. Or was a lawyer."

Roch looked up from his plate. "What do you mean?"

"I was fired," she explained, feeling slightly embarrassed and still pretty pissed. "Lawyers don't have a lot of time to be mothers. Or so my bosses believe."

"Well, that's bullshit," Ashe exclaimed, then

quickly turned to Soyala. "Sorry, honey. Mommy's a little upset about the issue of double standards."

"I'm actually thinking I'll go into solo practice," Lydia said after taking a sip of water. "Maybe a little office near where I live."

"In New Orleans," Roch said. It wasn't a question and his tone was anything but pleased. In fact it sounded pained.

"Of course, New Orleans," Ashe said, giving him an impatient look. "That's where she's from."

Roch's jaw tightened and he stabbed at a chunk of lasagna with his fork.

"Obviously there's a lot to consider," Lydia said, feeling the wave of tension in the air. It was the last thing she wanted to bring into Ashe and Raphael's home. "But if this baby is half Pantera, I would never cut the Wildlands or his species out of his life—"

"His?" Roch interrupted, his eyes cutting to her. They were a dark and stormy blue. "It's a male cub? How do you know?"

"I don't," she said, flustered by his quick passion. "I'm not sure why I said that."

"And there's no *if*, by the way," he added softly.

"What?" Her heart stalled and she looked around the room.

Roch glared at Raphael. "You didn't tell her?"

"Not officially," he uttered, uncomfortable.

"Oh, Raphael," Ashe scolded gently.

"I was easing my way into it."

Lydia was barely listening to them. Her heart was flickering hard in her chest, and her appetite was gone. "The tests are back? You know for certain…"

Raphael nodded. "Yes."

"Oh," she exclaimed. Her child was part Pantera. Her child would be a member of this tribe. It would be able to shift into a cat form like Roch. Her throat tightened. *A beautiful, powerful, remarkable cat, who might someday want to live here. Away from me.*

"Lydia, if I may," Raphael began gently. "How do you feel about the father having a relationship with the cub? If we can find him, of course. If you decide that you want the testing…"

"Do we need to talk about this now?" Roch put in darkly. He'd abandoned his food as well, and his eyes were pinned to Lydia's face.

"I don't know," she said, her voice reed-thin. "This is a lot to take in and I need to think about it." She put her napkin on her plate and eased her chair back. "I'm really tired."

"Of course you are," Ashe said with a quick and grim look at Raphael. "I'll walk you up, make sure you have everything you need."

"Thank you." She wasn't about to put up a fuss, or act like she could manage on her own. Granted, she probably could. But she kind of wanted Ashe with her. She looked at Raphael. "Good night."

"Sleep well, Lydia," he said gently, his eyes kind.

Then she glanced down at Roch. She

wanted to say something, but she wasn't sure what. *Don't leave? I need you? To talk to you? Be around you?* But she couldn't form the words. Or she was afraid of them. Vulnerability was a terrifying gift to give another person. But, lord help her, she wanted to give it to him. Like it or not—understand it or not—she had this connection to him that couldn't be explained or denied. And when their eyes caught and held, she saw in those incredible blue depths the same connection she felt for him mirrored back.

He gave her a tight smile, but said nothing. And after a moment, Lydia left the table with Ashe and headed upstairs to her room.

CHAPTER 6

The sound of a female's cries woke him. He stirred against the soft rug on the cold hardwood floor, lifted his head and stared at the woman on the bed. In the glow of the moonlight through the window to her left, he could see that she was sitting up, blond curls perfectly disheveled, tears falling down her cheeks. She'd had a nightmare. He could tell it was still affecting her; she was trembling. The ache to crawl up on the mattress and sit beside her, comfort her, was shockingly strong. But he'd sworn to remain where he was.

She swiped at her eyes, her tears, sniffed hard and took a breath. She would lie down again and slip back into sleep. He too was about to settle himself when her gaze dropped to the floor and she noticed him.

For the first time.

On the rug.

She screamed, her eyes flaring with shock and terror. Then she quickly covered her mouth, realizing it was him. No, not him.

His puma.

Roch scrambled to his feet—all four of them—and shifted into his male form. He hated himself for causing her fear after an obvious nightmare. He only wanted to bring her happiness. Make her feel safe. He went to her, the mattress dipping with his weight, and pulled her into his arms.

"I'm sorry," he whispered against her hair. "Christ, I'm sorry."

"What are you doing in here?" she whispered back. Still trembling, she clung to him.

"I don't know." But that was a lie. He knew. The need to be close to her, protect her, had driven him to wait outside Raphael and Ashe's place until the lights had gone out. Then he'd climbed up the side of the house and into her window. He'd known exactly where she was staying because he'd scented her.

His eyes slammed shut and he cursed silently.

He'd scented her.

Just as he had in New Orleans.

"I can't seem to walk away from you, Lydia," he said, his voice gravelly from sleep and from the quick shift. "I have no claim on you, and yet..."

"Yet what?" she whispered.

He dug deep for control as he held her. He was wearing the same thing he'd come to dinner in, but she wasn't. Clad in only a dark green tank top and underwear, she looked soft and sexy as hell, and he wanted her desperately. Her breasts pressed against his chest, and her nipples were hard.

His mouth watered.

"I need to touch you," he uttered impetuously. Before she could answer, he eased back so he could see her. Half of her beautiful face was cast in moonlight. Her eyes were huge and her lips were slightly swollen. He reached out and swiped at one lone and lasting tear near her cheekbone. "Your belly," he clarified gently. "Can I place my hand there?"

She looked confused. "Why, Roch?"

Yeah. Why indeed? "I can't explain it," he said, his eyes pinned to hers. *Don't want to explain.* "I just need to. Please."

She stared at him for a moment longer, breathing in, breathing out. Then she moved away. At first, Roch thought she was rejecting him. A wordless refusal. And could he blame her? His request was strange at best. But then she laid down, her head on her pillow, her hair fanned around her face, and lifted the tank top to just under her breasts.

Heat slammed into Roch, and his cock filled with blood. For a moment, he just looked her over. Hungrily, covetously, sweetly. Her incredible body streaked with moonlight. From her sexy toes painted a fiery red, to her long, luscious legs, up to a pair of pretty, almost girlish underwear. White with tiny strawberries. And then there was her belly. Tan and taut with just a hint of a swell.

Need raged through him. Never had he

wanted anything more. He lifted his gaze to meet hers. Clearly, she'd been watching him, and she gave him a gentle, encouraging smile. Christ, what he was doing—was this right?

"Come here, Roch," she said. "Lie down next to me. It's okay."

Her words and the warmth in her voice wrapped around him and squeezed. Shit. He'd never met anyone like her. It wasn't just that she was smart and strong and beautiful. That was amazing in and of itself. But she was also incredibly kind and warm. And he hadn't known—until that moment—that he truly craved those things. That he'd been missing those things in his life.

He stretched out beside her, inhaled her clean, floral scent, then laid his hand on her belly. He wasn't sure what he'd expected to happen in that moment. A sudden flash of insight, maybe? Or a blood-deep knowing that this woman and her cub belonged to him? But it wasn't either. Instead, a calming warmth suffused his skin. The kind of warmth that one liked to sit in for hours. A healing warmth. A happy, blissful warmth he'd never known existed. Or cared. Or had searched for.

She possessed that. In her heart and beneath her smooth skin.

Not wanting to hold her captive longer than she felt comfortable, or have her know how hard just being this close to her made him, Roch started to pull away. But Lydia covered his hand with hers. For a second he didn't move. His heart was slamming against his ribs, and every animal-like instinct he possessed wanted to pick her up and take her away. Maybe to his house. His bed. Claim her. Kill anything and everything that tried to get near.

But when she started slowly dragging his hand down toward her sex, his possessive instincts evaporated, and the desperate desire to mate took their place.

Lydia stopped when his fingers grazed the top of her strawberry underwear. The warmth from a moment ago—that delicate, gentle state of being—had already expanded into a ball of white-hot need within Roch and he needed to know if she felt it too. If she wanted his touch. Wanted his fingers inside of her? His mouth on her?

He lifted his gaze, and what he saw in those violet orbs was a depth of desire unlike anything he'd ever witnessed.

He growled softly at her, and her hand left his and went to his face. As her eyes melted into his, she brushed her fingers down one cheek and over his stubbled jaw. *Fuck them. Fuck them all.* He didn't care. At that moment, he didn't give a shit why he and Lydia were in Raphael and Ashe's house in the Wildlands— what challenges they faced outside in both their worlds. He just wanted to be with her, make her happy, and hot, and moan.

He followed the trail she'd set for him, slipping his fingers inside her panties. She lifted her chin and gasped when he cupped her.

"Oh, Lydia," he uttered, his skin going tight

around his muscles. "You're bare. Soft." He ran his thumb over the top of her sex. "I can feel your heat, how wet you are."

She licked her lips. "It's you," she whispered. "It's all you."

Her words made his heart expand. Whatever this was, between them, he wanted it. That sounded insane given how long they'd known one another. And yet, he was Pantera, and she was here with him in the magical Wildlands.

He slid one finger through her folds. It was so slick with cream he couldn't stop himself from entering her pussy. A groan rumbled in his chest and he felt his cock turn steel-hard.

She pressed herself against him and moaned. "More."

Every inch of him rigid with tension and hunger, Roch eased another finger inside her.

She groaned. "Yes. God, yes."

Did he want inside her? Fuck, yes. More than he wanted to live, at that moment. But he wasn't going there. Not now. Tonight was about her pleasure. He needed to see that. See her body writhe under his care. Hear her cries of climax as he stroked her.

"Roch," she uttered, canting her hips, trying to take him deeper.

"I'm here, Lydia," he said fiercely, as he deepened his thrusts.

I'm always going to be here. If you want me to be.

He pressed the pad of his thumb against her clit and she gasped.

Want me to be, Lydia. Fuck. Please, want me to be.

Her eyes closed and she gave herself over to his touch. He didn't rush her. Hell no. He wanted to watch this incredible display for as long as possible. Watch her hips circle and grind, listen to her breathing change as she neared climax.

Her nipples were hard points beneath her tank top, scraping against the fabric as her breasts moved, as her breathing grew rapid.

"Oh, god, Roch," she cried out softly. "I can't hold on..."

"You don't have to," he cooed. "Come for me."

It was the sweetest hell, watching her, touching her. Wanting to be inside of her. A wave of heat and cream bathed his fingers as he thrust hard and deep inside her. And when she moaned and thrashed her head from side to side against the pillow, he quickened the pace.

"Come for me, Lydia," he urged, circling her clit with his thumb.

"Oh, god," she rasped, her walls tightening and pulsating against his fingers.

Roch couldn't help himself. Couldn't stop himself. He dropped his head to her breast and suckled her nipple through the thin cotton.

She cried out, her hips jerking. Come leaked from the tip of Roch's painfully hard cock, but he could only think of her. He wanted that climax. He owned that climax.

As his thumb flicked her swollen clit, and his

tongue and teeth worked her nipple, he pressed hard against the sensitive spot inside her with the pads of his fingers.

"Oh, Roch," she cried out, writhing and moaning, coming apart under him. "Yes..."

His head swimming and his body roaring with unchecked desire, Roch lifted his head and watched her. Watched her ride each wave of orgasm as she rode his fingers. Watched her lips part and a cry emerge. She was so beautiful, so responsive. And he slowly thrust inside her until those glorious waves receded, until she couldn't move any more. Until she was so weary, she just stilled, and all he could hear was her rapid breathing.

Then he eased himself from her body. She looked spent, and for a moment he was worried. Was it all right to have touched her, made her come? Had he hurt her, or gods no—his heart seized—had he hurt the baby?

"Lydia." His voice was heavy with tension. "Are you okay? Did I hurt you?"

Her eyes opened and she blinked several times. Then she found his gaze and gave him the widest, most satisfied smile he'd ever seen. "Hurt me?" she laughed softly. "Roch?"

"Yes?"

That smile widened even further. "Hurt me some more?"

The apprehension left his body in a rush. Leaving only an intense hunger and a worrisome affection.

She reached for him, grabbed onto the waistband of his pants and tugged. Desire flooded his blood. But he put a hand over hers to stop her.

"No, Lydia." His voice was raw with tension. Fuck, he wanted her. Wanted to taste her. Bury himself within her.

She looked confused, pained. "Why? Don't you want me?" Her eyes dropped to his pants. "It looks like you want me."

"I want you more than I want to breathe or eat or see the sun set over the bayou for the rest of my life."

Her gaze returned to his. "Then..."

"I can't. Not yet." Not until I know who you belong to.

He hadn't said the words aloud, but she understood immediately, and her face fell.

"But I want to stay here with you," he said. "I need to. My cat and I are in agreement. But I'll return to the floor."

"That's silly," she said. "Don't go. I won't touch you."

"Christ, Lydia." She had no idea. She really didn't.

"I won't take advantage of you."

The teasing thread in her voice made him growl. He should say no. Should just leave the bed and park it on the rug. But he wasn't that strong. Not where she was concerned.

He lay back against the pillow and opened his arms to her. She went to him at once. And when he pulled her to him, she draped her thigh over his possessively.

"You slay me," he whispered against her

hair, feeling well, healthy and strong in his male form for the first time in days.

"And you make me feel safe."

His chest constricted. No one had ever said something like that to him. What was he going to do? How was he going to deal with the truth when it came?

He heard and felt her yawn and he pulled her even closer. "Sleep now. I'm not going anywhere."

He closed his eyes too and tried to calm his breathing. After a few minutes, he thought she was asleep. But then she whispered, "Roch?"

"Mmm hmm?"

"Do you think it's true?"

Without even a hesitation, he knew what she meant. "That this cub is mine?"

"Yes."

"I don't know, Lydia." But I want it to be. Goddess help me, I want it to be.

When she didn't say anything in reply, he kissed her hair and stroked her back. And when her breathing evened out, and her limbs grew still, he let his mind go, too. And he followed her into sleep.

Lydia woke to the warmth of the early morning sun on her face and the feeling of a man's thickly muscled arms around her. As she opened her eyes and took stock of her surroundings, she blushed with pleasure. Most of the bedding was either on the floor or on its way there. She was completely wrapped around Roch's side and her underwear was still wet.

Her belly, and pretty much everything south of it, clenched. Last night had been extraordinary, to say the least. Her breath caught as she remembered his hands on her, *in* her. And her heart kicked as she recalled his reticence to make love to her.

Maybe that was a momentary hiccup. Maybe today will be different.

She lifted her head and let her eyes move over him. He was so beautiful, so...male. She reached up and dragged a thick lock of his blond hair away from his eyes. Tan skin, sharp angles, stubbled jaw, hard neck, powerful, wide shoulders.

Yes. Today will be different.

Without thinking, she leaned in and pressed her lips to his neck. One gentle kiss. Then she eased back an inch and swiped at his pulse point with her tongue. Oh, he tasted so good.

It was the only thought she could manage before she heard a growl and was swiftly rolled to her back.

She gasped and stared up at the male who had stolen her heart but had yet to take control of it. He looked fearsome and sexy, his eyes blue pools of sleepy hunger, as he easily held himself just inches above her.

"What was that, Ms. Page?" he said on a playful growl.

Her gaze moved from his eyes down to his

lips. "I believe I was overcome with the need to taste you."

He groaned, then lowered his head and kissed her. A soft, deep, teasing kiss that went on for a good five minutes and inflamed every inch of her.

"How's that?" he asked confidently.

"How was what?" she said, deadpan.

His brows lowered. "I kissed you, woman."

"Oh, come on now. I'll need so much more than that to give my opinion." She grinned and pushed him off her—pushed him to his back.

Granted, Roch was pretty much built like a slab of iron. He could've easily remained where he was. But he let her direct him, let her do what was comfortable for her body. And lord, what was comfortable for her was being on top of him, straddling him, feeling his long, hard muscles—especially the one between his legs.

His gaze moved up her body, then settled on her face. A wicked gleam lit in his extraordinary blue eyes. "Take advantage of me, Lydia."

It was from their conversation the night before, she realized, grinning. She liked him this way. Playful and sexual, and not too serious. She leaned over and kissed him, her palms on either side of his head—her hair falling around them like a coiled curtain. Roch may have been a gentleman up until that point, trying to keep himself and his hunger under control. But once she started in on his mouth, kissing and licking his lips, nipping and suckling his tongue, he went wild. His hands came around to cup her backside possessively, squeezing the flesh as he groaned.

"I can't get enough of you," he uttered against her mouth. "Never enough."

They kissed hard and impassioned, ground their lower halves against one another, made out like teenagers with only stolen moments in the back of one of their parents' cars.

Her underwear soaked and her mouth desperate to taste the rest of him, Lydia sat up and pulled her tank over her head. After she tossed it to the floor, she found Roch's gaze once again. As he took her in, he looked like his puma. Or the male equivalent of it. Fierce, hungry, unable to quell its instincts. As in...if the puma wanted something, he took it.

And lord, she sure hoped he took it.

Her hands went to the front of his pants. She traced the outline of his cock, her mouth dropping open as she took in his extraordinary length. Her sex tingled in anticipation. Oh, she wanted him inside of her.

Roch reached for her then, palming her breasts. Massaging. Giving them a hard squeeze, before gently pinching each of her nipples.

"I want you," she told him on an impatient moan. "Inside of me. Please, Roch."

His eyes flashed fire. "I can't. Fuck, I can't take you, no matter how badly I want you."

"Why?" This was madness. What was he trying to prove?

In the soft light of morning, he looked doubly fierce. "You don't belong to me."

Was it possible for a heart to hurt and swell at the same time? she wondered. "I decide who I belong to, Roch." She slipped her hand inside his pants and wrapped her fingers around his shaft.

"Damn you," he growled, his hips jacking up.

"No. Damn you. Do you think I want to touch anyone else like this?"

That did it. Roch went crazy at her words. Growling, groaning, grabbing her hips and grinding her sex into the base of his cock. Over and over.

Until a knock sounded on the door.

Both of them froze.

"Lydia?" It was Ashe, in her lovely singsong voice. "You awake? I have breakfast downstairs if you're interested."

Lydia's eyes flew to Roch. He looked murderous. Like he might actually turn into his cat and attack.

"No hurry," Ashe continued. "But there are beignets. They make the best beignets here in the Wildlands."

With a nearly inaudible curse, Roch lifted her up and placed her down on the mattress. He was off the bed in seconds, running his hands through his hair. He looked wild and gorgeous.

"I'm awake," Lydia called out, worried Roch would do something foolish. Like snarl at the woman to get lost. "Sounds good. I'll be down in a few minutes."

"Okay, great!"

Lydia waited for the sound of the woman's footfall to disappear before she turned back to Roch.

"Don't go," she said to him. "Stay and have breakfast."

"That wouldn't be wise," he said, jaw tight. He wasn't looking at her. Anywhere but at her. Playful Roch was gone.

"Why not? You were here for dinner."

"I'm in no mood to be sociable. Besides, I've got to get home, shower and change before work." He turned to her then and stilled. For several long seconds, he took her in. Her eyes, her mouth, her naked torso. "You truly are the most beautiful woman, Lydia."

Her heart melted like a damn ice cream cone in the sun. She reached for him. "Stay."

"I can't." But he went to her anyway and kissed her. It wasn't a hungry, desire-filled kiss. It was more like a goodbye.

When he pulled away, Lydia couldn't help herself. She had to ask him. "Do you want to know, Roch? About the cub?"

Dread glistened in his blue eyes. "Of course I do, but—"

"You're scared?" she finished.

"Fuck, Lydia, of course I'm scared."

She scooted to the edge of the bed. "I'm scared too. Everything's changed for me. In the blink of an eye. My whole life. Where do I belong? What do I do?"

He sighed. "You will always belong here if that's what you want."

"What do you want?"

His jaw looked so tight Lydia was afraid it might crack. "You don't understand. The ways of a Pantera male are very different than that of a man. We have honor. A code we live by. But more important than that is the fact that our kind can finally, after fifty years, reproduce. We can continue." He took a deep breath. "This cub..."

"Is very important," she said.

"Yes." He was silent for a moment, then, "I have to go."

She didn't put up a fight this time. She understood the gravity of the situation. Love didn't or couldn't always trump practicality and allegiance. She may not have liked it. But she understood it.

"How are you planning to get out without anyone noticing?" she asked.

"Same way I came in." He gave her a small smile. "Have a beignet for me?"

She returned it. "Sure."

Then watched him go out the window with the supreme grace of the cat who dwelled inside of him.

CHAPTER 7

"Nothing?" Roch said incredulously. "No samples? No files?"

"How's that possible?" Damien asked in between bites of ham sandwich. "Did they search the entire facility?"

Raphael glanced up from his laptop. They were gathered in his private office inside Suit headquarters. "Not exactly. They were stopped before they could search the basement."

"Stopped?" Roch repeated, leaning back against the window. "By who?"

"The man who supposedly owns The Haymore Center. A Stanton Locke." He returned his gaze to the screen of his computer. "I put a few of the Geeks on it, and it seems Mr. Locke has friends in very high places. From politicians to celebrities to law enforcement. One of our Hunters was actually taken to a humans' jail."

"Holy shit," Damien exclaimed, putting down his sandwich and taking out his iPhone. "Which one?"

"Keira. She was protecting Reny."

"Sebastian's mate?"

Raphael nodded. "With her experience in the FBI we thought she'd be an asset in the field. She was. Until she saw this Locke bastard. She was convinced she knew the man. Wouldn't stop with the questions. When he got pissed and grabbed her arm, Keira stepped in. And you know Keira."

"Ballbuster," Roch said, crossing his arms over his chest. "Best Hunter I've ever known."

"Damn right. NOLA PD showed up pretty quick after that and Locke said Keira attacked him."

"What a pussy, and not the good kind," Damien said with a rare growl. "Is she still in jail?"

"No. Sebastian got her released. He headed to New Orleans the second he heard about Reny. They're all on their way back now."

Roch turned to face the window and the view of the meadow where the Pantera took meals together. "With nothing." In one sense he was relieved that there was no file on Lydia. If it got leaked to the human press that she was carrying a Pantera cub, she'd never be able to live easily outside of the Wildlands. Not that he wanted her to. Shit, he really didn't want her to. But with no records, no samples, no nothing, it was going to be near to impossible to track down any women who may have been given a Pantera sample.

"I say we question Hiss about this Stanton Locke, see what he knows," Damien suggested.

"You really think there's a connection?" Raphael asked.

Roch glanced over his shoulder, watched as the newbie Suit warred with himself on how to handle his leader's question. Finally Damien said, "I think it's worth a shot. If anything, I'll see how his eyes change, and his expression, when I ask him."

Raphael didn't contemplate this idea very long. "Do it. Head over to Medical."

"Now?" The male's eyes widened. "Alone?"

"You can handle it."

Damien tried like hell not to grin like a Pantera young, but it was impossible. He nodded at Raphael, and quickly left the room.

"That was nice," Roch said, pushing away from the window and walking over to Raphael's desk.

"Nothing nice about it," he replied. "He's going to be a formidable Suit. Just wanted him to find his balls and speak up."

Roch laughed. Then he dropped into the chair opposite his boss. "You think Hiss might know this guy?"

Raphael lifted his shoulders in a shrug. "My guess is no. I think Hiss is telling the truth when he says he was working with Shakpi's disciples. Don't think Locke has any connection there. But who the hell knows?"

"We need to find those samples," Roch said darkly.

"Damn right, we do. We can't have Pantera cubs being born outside the Wildlands. They're too important to the survival of our species."

The male's words raked through Roch. Lydia's cub. They needed to protect it. They needed to know who had sired it. He needed to know. Or Christ, did he? Would it truly make a difference? Now, or six months from now, or ten years from now? Would anybody remember, or care? And would she care?

"Just because they found no samples with the words Puma Shifter written on them doesn't mean they're not there," Roch put in.

"I know." Raphael lowered his voice even though they were the only two males in the room. Outside his door was a group of Diplomats, and some of the Geeks, working on a variety of issues. Including the very one they were discussing now.

"I didn't want to say this in front of the rookie," he began. "But we still have two Hunters inside. And when the lights go out and the alarm goes on, they'll continue their search."

Roch sat back, impressed. "You're damn good at keeping secrets, boss."

"Back at you, brother." Raphael too, leaned back in his chair.

"What does that mean?"

Raphael's brows lifted. "Loved that lasagna so much you came back for seconds?"

"You knew I was there."

The head of the Suits laughed, closed his laptop. "Are you really asking me if I knew someone was in my home with my mate and cub?"

Right. That was a pretty stupid question. Of

course, Raphael and Ashe had been the last things on his mind last night. Or this morning. "And you allowed it?"

After a heavy exhale, the male said, "I am hoping..." He shrugged. "Ashe is hoping."

"For what?"

Green-gold eyes flashed with interest. "We want the woman to remain here. With her cub. You have a connection to her. A need to be around her constantly. It's like my connection to Ashe. And to Soyala. It's impossible to turn from. It's all-consuming."

Roch growled softly. "Yes."

"And you want her to stay."

"I want her, period," Roch ground out. "But what if the cub isn't mine?"

"Will it matter to you?"

"Of course not. I would claim it if she'd let me. But that's not the point. You know how we are, Raphael. Do you think a Pantera male would allow me to get close to the female carrying his young?"

That question weighed on the Suit leader. He scrubbed a hand over his chin. "It could cause a problem."

"Try a fight to the death." Because as much as he wouldn't want to rip any of his Pantera brothers apart, Roch was pretty sure he wouldn't be able to watch another male touch her.

Christ, just the thought of it made his cat feral.

"And fuck." He hadn't thought about what Lydia might want. "What if *she* wants this other male in her life?" *I lose my damn mind completely.*

"She wants you," Raphael said with a snort. "Shit, we all heard how much she wants you."

Roch snarled at him. "Don't make me make you fire my ass."

Raphael laughed. "What is the answer to this then, my friend?"

"The truth?"

"They say it sets you free," Raphael remarked.

At several points in his life, Roch would've appreciated that answer. Reveled in it even. But not today. Today there was nothing he wanted less than to be free. Of Lydia Page or the tiny life growing inside of her.

With a bluff of rugged hillside to her left and a curve of mysterious caves to her right, Lydia felt as though she was in a foreign land. Not that she'd been to all that many foreign lands. But she could imagine.

Thick, gloriously green vegetation hung from the rocks above her and rested languidly on the surface of the warm water of the bayou pool she was swimming in.

A bayou pool.

Never in a million years would she have thought she'd be doing this. *And* doing it buck-naked with three other women.

But seriously, that's what "recently fired, recently discovered by a puma shifter and brought to a magical spot in the bayous of Louisiana" people did, right?

"Are you sure Keira and Bayon aren't going to be around today?" Julia asked Genevieve with a quick glance at the beginnings of the couple's new home that was being built near the caves above them.

A Diplomat, Genevieve Burel was the Nurturer Jean-Baptiste's mate. She was a gorgeous blonde with pale blue eyes and a friendly smile. And she'd welcomed Lydia into the circle of friends like they'd known each other for years.

"Positive," Genevieve told her. "They're both on assignment."

"Top secret stuff?" Julia asked.

"If I told you I'd have to kill you."

Ashe and Lydia laughed while Julia splashed the female. Genevieve grinned and swam backwards toward a small alcove under a thick patch of greenery.

Growing up, Lydia had several close friends. But after high school, they'd grown apart. And well, she hadn't tried to make more. There just hadn't been time. Or maybe that had been an excuse not to get close to people. Fear of losing them again, or something. She had the same fear when it came to a certain Pantera male.

She looked at the women around her now, and wondered if there was truly a place for her here.

"Well this is very decadent." Ashe remarked before diving beneath the water and emerging five feet away with a wide grin.

"We all deserve a little decadence," Julia put in, making small circles on the surface of the pool with her index finger. "Especially the new mama."

"I can't tell you how excited I am for you," Genevieve said, swimming over. "It means there's hope for us here. To bring more Pantera cubs into the world."

It was shocking how different the reaction to her pregnancy was here in the Wildlands versus out in the wilds of New Orleans. Where the Pantera saw her half human, half shifter baby as a blessing, the assholes at Haymore had seen it as a terrible mistake. How would the rest of the world react, she wondered. And would she find out sooner rather than later? After all, she'd only agreed to stay here for a few days.

Her heart seized in her chest at the thought of leaving.

No. At the thought of leaving *him*.

"How long has it been since a Pantera cub was born?" Lydia asked.

"Not counting Soyala?" Ashe said. "Over fifty years."

"There was a curse put on our species," Genevieve explained. "Soyala changed all of that."

Curiosity pushed her to ask, "How?"

"Females," came a male voice at the shore. "Remain below the water, please."

Genevieve gasped and submerged herself to her neck, Ashe grabbed a piece of water plant and placed it in front of her, and Julia remained where she was, her eyes narrowing on the man—the male—standing on the bank.

"Roch, how the hell did you know where we were?" Ashe demanded. Then she glanced over at Lydia and sniffed. "Never mind."

Lydia stared at him. Standing there in a pair of faded jeans and a white t-shirt. She mentally sighed. The guy could sport casual or career and he would always be the sexiest male in the room.

Or the bayou.

His eyes, those summer sky blue eyes, captured hers. "I need to speak to you."

"Hey Roch, we're swimming here," Julia called out. "You know, girl time."

"Yeah, go back to the house, Roch, and wait for her there," Ashe said, though her tone was far from dictatorial.

"No." He said the word to them, but his eyes remained on Lydia.

As Lydia was held captive by his hot stare, Julia and Genevieve groaned simultaneously.

"If you hang out here and any of our mates see you they're going to kill you," Julia said, then turned to Lydia and explained. "Sounds uncivilized and barbaric, but there it is. It's what you sign up for if you get with any of our males, FYI."

Lydia nodded, but decided not to say that the idea of an uncivilized and barbaric Roch was intriguing as hell.

"She's not going for any of our males," Roch said tightly.

"Someone's acting a little possessive," Genevieve remarked. "Especially over a female who doesn't belong to him."

"Lydia," he called to her, ignoring the women's barbs. "Please."

"I'm not kidding about our mates, Roch," Julia called out.

He growled, and for the first time, he turned and glared at each woman in turn. "Let them come."

"Oh Jesus," Julia uttered.

The last thing Lydia wanted was for him to get into a fight. Get hurt. That gorgeous face did not need any bruises. "I'm coming," she called, then started swimming toward him. When she was ten feet from shore, she stopped and addressed him. "What's wrong?"

He looked tense. "I need to say something to you."

"We can talk back at Ashe's—"

"No. It can't wait."

She glanced behind her, then back at him. "Even for some privacy?"

"I'm not ashamed of what I have to say, Lydia." He came to the very edge of the water and dropped onto his haunches. His jeans hugged tight to his muscular thighs, and the white t-shirt strained against smooth, tanned, muscle. "Have the testing done."

Surprise caught and held her. "Roch..."

"We need to know the truth."

"We?" She held her breath.

"You, me, the Pantera."

A tight knot forming in her throat, she swam

closer. "What if it's another male's—"

"Then the male should know." His nostrils flared, but he continued. "It's not about you and me anymore. It's about the Pantera. Pack first. The cub is what's important here. The cub and its safety is everything to our species."

Lydia stared at him, her heart pricked and bleeding inside her chest. Yes, she was grateful for what he was saying, how he felt about her child. But gone was his fight. For her. Or for the male who might try and claim her.

Pain lashed through her, but she pushed it away. It was important to know. Her value and importance was in her cub.

"That's what I came to say." He stood up, nodded to the females in the water. "I apologize, and will speak to each of your mates."

As he shifted into his puma and took off up the hillside, Ashe, Genevieve and Julia all surrounded her. They didn't say anything, but they didn't have to. It was something all females understood and sympathized with— Pantera or human. The pain of rejection.

CHAPTER 8

He despised himself.

He despised everyone around him, too.

It was a good thing that the one male Roch had told about his adventure to the bayou pool happened to be a Nurturer. Because as soon as Jean-Baptiste had given him the black eye he'd deserved, the male had quickly set about treating it.

Roch stalked through town in his puma state, a file folder between his teeth. According to Damien, Hiss had claimed to know nothing about the human male, Locke. But Roch had done some unconventional research on the man with Xavier, the head of the Geeks. Locke had been a foundling, taken in by a very rich man. A man who was rarely seen and rumored to be gravely ill. Seemed that Locke was devoted to him. Among his vast holdings, The Haymore Center was one of several research and/or medical facilities he owned. And though they offered a wide range of infertility options including egg donation, testing and surgery, it looked as though experimentation was their primary focus.

Cell and tissue rejuvenation, to be exact.

His jaw clamped a little tighter around the file as he leapt over a stretch of stream bordering Raphael and Ashe's property. He needed to talk to his boss.

"Afternoon, Suit."

Roch's puma whirled around and stalked forward, toward the voice. Which belonged to none other than Parish. The leader of the Hunters wore a dark, irritated expression. So he'd gotten Roch's text. In seconds, Roch shifted into his male form.

The golden eyed male looked him over and sneered. "Only one black eye? I think you might need a set."

Right. Baptiste might have a genius at healing, but only time erased the bruising. Roch raised his arms in surrender. "Have at it, Parish."

The male sniffed, even kicked a rock with the tip of his boot. "Shit, brother, it's not as much fun when you welcome it."

"Look, I needed to speak with Lydia. It was the only way."

Parish was silent for a moment, then he lifted his shoulders and shrugged, the wind of battle now calm. "Well, I hope it was worth it."

Worth it? Seeing the look on her face when he'd made it pretty damn clear the cub was the most important thing to him, to the Pantera?

His jaw went tight. He truly despised himself today.

"Hey, if it wasn't," Parish put in, running a hand through his long, dark hair. "Or you didn't get what you needed, you can try again. She's over at Medical right now."

Roch's heart dropped like a stone into his gut. "What?"

"With my fully-clothed mate."

Shit. "Did you see what she was doing? Why she was there?"

The Hunter studied him, dark brows descending over those gold eyes. "Paternity test. She wanted to get it done today, as she's heading back to New Orleans in the morning."

The blood drained from Roch's body. He'd told her to get the testing. He just hadn't believed it would be right away.

"I know I shouldn't give a shit after the near-visuals in the bayou pool," Parish began reluctantly. "But are you all right?

Hell no he wasn't all right. He'd made a huge mistake. If he lost the woman he—

With a growl, he shifted back into his puma. After a quick nod to Parish, he scooped up the file in his teeth and took off toward Raphael's place. Not just to give him the information he'd found, but to ask him—and his mate—for help.

Her heart beating wildly in her chest, Lydia stood on the porch of Roch's home. It was a lovely two-story Craftsman-style house, more modern than any of the dwellings she'd seen in the Wildlands. And it suited him perfectly. That warm, sexy, cerebral style.

As her hand rose to the door she wondered once again why Raphael had asked her to bring some paperwork over to Roch's place. Of course, she was happy to do it. Anything for the couple who were treating her like an honored guest. But in her gut, she knew it had to be an excuse to get her here. The only question was, who had the idea? And why?

After knocking, she stepped back and waited. It wasn't long before the door opened and the sunset behind her revealed the most gorgeous male in the universe. Her heart squeezed with love and trepidation.

His face split into a wide grin. He wasn't surprised to see her. In fact, he looked pleased.

She held out a large envelope. "I brought this from Raphael."

"Thanks." He took it from her, then stepped back. "Come on in."

"I should get back."

His eyes moved over her face. "Please, Lydia."

Resisting this male was like trying to resist air or light or water. He felt so strangely essential to her being.

The moment she stepped inside, she felt at home. Not that she was going to say that out loud. Instead, as she took in all the refinished wood, modern, yet comfortable furnishings and windows, windows, windows, she said, "I like your house."

"I like you in it," he said, taking her hand.

Lydia's breath caught in her throat. What was this? What was he saying?

"Come on," he continued with a soft smile, leading her out of the foyer. "I'll show you around."

Confused, yet happy in a way she could never explain, his hand holding hers, she followed him through several rooms. Kitchen, dining area, a back porch overlooking a small pond. It was all unfussy and gorgeous and clever. Like him. When he led her down another hallway and she spotted bedrooms, she wondered if she was going to get a look at where he slept. The idea made her blush and grin. But the bedroom he led her into wasn't his own.

"What's this?" she asked, suddenly breathless as she took in the lovely white crib, changing table, and pale green rocking chair.

"It's just a few things," he began, his voice low and deep and threaded with hope. "I thought maybe you'd want to choose colors and how everything is arranged. And if you don't like any of this, we can get something else. Maybe an animal theme..."

She turned to look at him. "I don't understand."

Ice blue eyes that were filled with only warmth and want stared back at her. "For the cub, Lydia."

"What you said today—"

He groaned. "I was an asshole. A male so deeply in love with a female he felt he didn't have the right to claim, he got scared."

Lydia's entire body erupted with heat, and her breath was locked inside her lungs. But she managed to push out a hopeful, "And now?"

He laughed, his eyes crinkling with affection. "Now he doesn't give a fuck. He wants her. He loves her. He's going to claim her, no matter what."

Lydia stood there, in the bedroom this male had declared was her child's. He'd told her he loved her, that he wanted her. And she could see it in his eyes. But she still had to know...

"I had the test performed today," she said.

Not a flash of concern crossed his handsome features. He only grinned at her. So happy. So confident. So sure.

"I don't care what it said, Lydia. I want you. I want this cub. I will be a strong, available father to it." He reached for her. "And if another male tries to claim you and the cub, we'll deal with it. No bluster. No fight." He lifted his chin and smiled. "We may be puma shifters, but we will be civilized and supportive."

It was all she needed to hear. It was everything. She went to him and wrapped her arms around his waist. Looked up into his beautifully fierce face. "I love your eyes."

He chuckled softly. "And I love you."

She squeezed him tighter. "I hope our baby gets them."

It was as if the air rushed out of the room. Those eyes she loved widened and Roch uttered hoarsely, "What did you say?"

The happiness that filled her in that moment was unlike anything she had ever experienced.

She smiled up at him. "Just that I hope our cub has your—"

"Ours?" He didn't let her answer. His head dropped and his mouth covered hers.

Lydia wrapped her arms around his neck and kissed him back, so fiercely, so lovingly, both of them groaned with the pleasure of it.

She was in love. Deeply and desperately. With the father of her child. How in the world was such a miracle possible?

Roch eased her down to the carpet and started taking off her clothes. Her skin prickling with heat and excitement, Lydia helped him. Especially when it was time to undress him. She just wanted them naked and in each other's arms where they belonged. And when he stretched out over her, his hard muscle against her soft flesh, she sighed with ecstasy.

The magic of the Wildlands was here, with her and inside her. And she was never going to let it go.

As Roch took her mouth again, she wrapped her legs around his waist and lifted her hips in invitation. She wasn't going to play coy—she'd waited too long to know what he would feel like inside her. And when he entered her with one deep, hungry thrust, she cried out in both pleasure and intensity. He was long and thick and hot, and her walls instantly welcomed him, bathing him in cream.

Desperate for him to move, Lydia circled her hips. But Roch pressed her down into the soft carpet and held her there with unspoken authority and strength.

She looked up at him. "What's wrong?"

He gazed down at her with eyes so filled with hunger and love, her heart contracted. "This will sound insane."

"Tell me."

"We didn't get to make our cub this way..."

Pain, beautiful pain erupted within her. "Oh, Roch," she said on a sigh. "The next one. Our next one."

"Yes, but..." He eased out of her and thrust back in.

She gasped with pleasure. So filled. So desperate for more. Him. All of him.

"Can we pretend that we are?" he asked, lowering his head and nipping at her bottom lip. "Can we pretend that when I come inside you, when you cry out and take your release, and I follow you there, that we're making our—"

"Son," she said, tears pricking her eyes. She nodded. "Oh god, Roch. I love you. Yes."

He said nothing more. His mouth covered hers, and as he kissed her deeply, lovingly, he thrust inside her. Taking her to heaven. Building the heat and intensity within her.

Lydia wrapped her arms around him and held on tight. She wasn't going to last long. Roch was so big, so hard, the head of his cock rubbing deliciously against the spot inside her pussy that triggered her climax.

And when he ripped his mouth from hers and buried it in her neck, suckling, scraping his teeth against her pulse point, she exploded.

Crying out, she came. Her walls milking him

until he too snarled and bucked and took his release.

It was moments—minutes, hours?—until he stopped thrusting inside her, until they cooled. But when they did, Roch eased to his back and pulled her in close. Satiated, Lydia snuggled against him. On the soft carpet. She smiled against his shoulder. On the floor of their cub's bedroom.

"Tell me you're not going back to New Orleans," he said with a possessive rasp to his tone. "Except to get your things."

Her heart stuttered. "You know about that?"

"Tell me, Lydia. Please. Before I lose my mind. I'm in love with you. I think I have been ever since you offered me your beignet."

She smiled and kissed his shoulder. This male made her deliriously happy.

"Tell me," he growled.

"I'll stay," she laughed. "Of course I'll stay."

He heaved an enormous sigh. "Christ, I'm glad. But you know, it's not enough."

She lifted her head, her heart jumping in her blood now. "What do you mean?"

He looked calm, satiated, tousled. Gorgeous. His eyes connected with hers and held. "You know about mating. Ashe and Julia and others too, I'm sure, have explained our ways."

She nodded, breath held. "It's like a human marriage."

He shook his head. "No, Lydia. It's deeper than that. Truer. It is a bond that lasts not just a lifetime, but beyond."

"Well, that's a good thing," she said with genuine feeling. "I love that."

His eyes moved over her face. "And I love you." He reached around her naked ass and yanked her to him.

She squealed.

"Will you be my mate, Lydia Page?" he asked in the most serious tone she'd ever heard from him. "Live with me, sleep with me, make love with me, laugh with me?" His eyes flashed with sudden humor. "Let me share in diaper duties for our son?"

It wasn't possible to be any happier than she was, but with that question—no, that proposal—she truly thought she'd died and gone to heaven. She was deeply and truly loved by the male who had given her a son.

"Is that a yes, Ms. Page?" he said with playful ferocity.

She smiled. "That, my gorgeous Pantera male—my mate—is an absolutely, definitely, love you, yes, yes, yes."

He kissed her, soft and gentle, then eased her onto her back.

"What are you doing?" she asked with a girlish giggle.

Up on his hands and knees and headed for the lower half of her body, looking as near to his puma as possible in his male form, Roch snarled sensually at her.

"I say we seal this with a kiss," he uttered, his breath near her belly now.

"My lips are up here, Roch," she said breathlessly, watching him, waiting.

His eyes went heavy lidded as he grasped her inner thighs and splayed them wide. "Not the lips I'm hungry for at the moment."

And as he proved that statement, all Lydia could do was sigh.

EPILOGUE

Three days later

"Rosalie is home, but Mercier is dead," Raphael said to the small group of Hunters, Suits and Nurturers who were gathered in his office at Diplomatic headquarters. It was night, and they'd been at it for hours. "And our Hunters inside Haymore haven't reported back."

Sebastian cursed. "This new enemy is worse than the last."

"But what is it they want?" Genevieve asked, nonplussed.

"Our DNA," Roch said, glancing around the dimly lit room with its half empty plates and endless water bottles. "We don't know why yet. What they hope to use it for. But it has something to do with that Stanton Locke and the mysterious man he cares for. As you know, my mate is an attorney and she's calling all her contacts, trying to get a hold of Stanton's financial dealings. What, how much, with whom."

"Please stop saying that bastard's name," Keira ground out from her spot on the edge of Raphael's desk. "Do you know what he said when the cops hauled me away? 'Pantera are dangerous creatures.' He wants us all rounded up so human society can be safe."

"That piece of shit will come to know how unsafe we are," Xavier muttered. He turned to Raphael. "What do we do?"

The leader of the Suits looked at each one of them and sighed. "Maybe it's time to get on camera and speak. Tell the truth. Let the humans see us."

A slate grey puma burst into the room and snarled at the lot of them. In seconds, it shifted and revealed a very pissed-off Parish.

"What is it?" Raphael demanded.

"The elders are with Hiss, as he asked," the leader of the Hunters said with a sneer. "They are giving him the chance to confess what he knows."

"The three are visiting a prisoner?" Keira exclaimed, coming to her feet. "What the hell is happening?"

"Oh," Parish continued. "And we have photographers at our borders."

Calmly, every bit the formidable Diplomat he was, Raphael stood up and walked out from behind his desk. "Roch, I'll need to borrow your tie. Looks like our time on camera has come sooner than we thought."

OTHER BOOKS BY LAURA WRIGHT

Mark of the Vampire
Book 1: Eternal Hunger
Book 2: Eternal Kiss
Book 2.5: Eternal Blood (Especial)
Book 3: Eternal Captive
Book 4: Eternal Beast
Book 4.5: Eternal Beauty (Especial)
Book 5: Eternal Demon
Book 6: Eternal Sin

Bayou Heat Series
Raphael & Parish (1 & 2)
Bayon & Jean-Baptiste(3 & 4)
Talon & Xavier (5 & 6)
Sebastian & Aristide (7 & 8)

Wicked Ink Chronicles
First Ink
Shattered Ink

ABOUT THE AUTHOR

New York Times and *USA Today* best selling author **Laura Wright** has spent most of her life immersed in acting, singing and competitive ballroom dancing. When she found the world of writing and books and endless cups of coffee, she knew she was home. Laura is the author of the Mark of the Vampire series, Bayou Heat series, Wicked Ink Chronicles, and the upcoming Cavanaugh Brothers series. She lives in Los Angeles with her husband, two young children, and three lovable dogs. Visit her website at laurawright.com.

Excerpt from

HUNT THE DARKNESS

BY ALEXANDRA IVY

Guardians of Eternity Series
Released May 28, 2014

CHAPTER 1

Northern Canada

Roke hadn't yet given into his overwhelming desire to commit gargoyle-cide.

But it was a near thing.

Roke was anti-social by nature, and having to endure the endless chatter from a stunted gargoyle for the past three weeks had been nothing short of torture.

It was only the fact that Levet could sense Yannah, the demon who'd helped Sally flee from Chicago, that kept him from sending the annoying twit back to Styx.

His mating connection to Sally meant that he could sense her, but with Yannah's ability to teleport from one place to another in a blink of an eye meant by the time he could locate her, she was already gone.

Levet seemed to have a more direct connection to Yannah, although they still spent their nights chasing from one place to another, always one step behind them.

Until tonight.

With a small smile he came to a halt, allowing his senses to flow outward.

The sturdy cottage tucked on the eastern coast of British Columbia was perched to overlook the churning waves of the North Pacific Ocean. Built from the gray stones that lined the craggy cliffs it had a steep, metal roof to shed the heavy snowfalls and windows that were already shuttered against the late autumn breeze. A handful of outhouses surrounded the bleak property, but it was far enough away from civilization to avoid prying eyes.

Not that prying eyes could have detected him.

Leaving his custom-built turbine powered motorcycle hidden in the distant town, Roke was dressed in black. Black jeans, black tee and black leather jacket with a pair of knee high moccasins that allowed him to move in lethal silence.

With his bronzed skin and dark hair that brushed his broad shoulders, he blended into the darkness with ease. Only his eyes were visible.

Although silver in color, they were so pale they appeared white in the moonlight, and rimmed by a circle of pure black.

Over the centuries those eyes had unnerved the most savage demons. No one liked the sensation that their soul was being laid bare.

On the other hand, his lean, beautiful features that were clearly from Native

American origins had been luring women to his bed since he'd awoken as a vampire.

They sighed beneath the touch of his full, sensual lips and eagerly pressed to the lean, chiseled perfection of his body. Their fingers traced the proud line of his nose, the wide brow, and his high cheekbones.

It didn't matter that most considered him as cold and unfeeling as a rattlesnake. Or that he would sacrifice anything or anyone to protect his clan.

They found his ruthless edge...exciting.

All except one notable exception.

A damned shame that exception happened to be his mate.

Roke grimaced.

No. Not mate.

Or at least, not in the traditional sense.

Three weeks ago he'd been in Chicago when the demon-world had battled against the Dark Lord. They'd managed to turn back the hordes of hell, but instead of allowing him to return to his clan in Nevada, Styx, the Anasso (King of all Vampires) had insisted that he remain to babysit Sally Grace, a witch who'd fought with the Dark Lord.

Roke had been furious.

Not only was he desperate to return to his people, but he hated witches.

All vampires did.

Magic was the one weapon they had no defense against.

Regrettably, when Styx gave an order, a wise vampire jumped to obey.

The alternative wasn't pretty.

Of course, at the time none of them had realized that Sally was half demon. Or that she would panic at being placed in the dungeons beneath Styx's elegant lair.

He absently rubbed his inner forearm where the mating mark was branded into his skin.

The witch claimed that she was simply trying to enchant him long enough to convince him to help her escape. And after his initial fury at realizing her demon magic had somehow ignited the mating bond, Roke had grudgingly accepted it had been an accident.

What he hadn't accepted was her running off to search for the truth of her father.

Dammit.

It was her fault they were bound together.

She had no right to slip away like a thief in the night.

"Do you sense anyone?"

The question was spoken in a low voice that was edged with a French accent, jerking Roke out of his dark broodings. Glancing downward, he ruefully met his companion's curious gaze

What the hell had happened to his life?

A mate that wasn't a mate. A three foot gargoyle side-kick. And a clan that had been without their chief for far too long.

"She's there," he murmured, his gaze skimming over the creature's ugly mug. Levet had all the usual gargoyle features. Gray skin, horns, a small snout, and a tail he kept lovingly polished. It was only his delicate wings and diminutive size that marked him as different.

Oh, and his appalling lack of control over his magic. He turned back to the cottage where he could catch the distinctive scent of peaches. A primitive heat seared through him, drawing him forward. "I have you, little witch."

Scampering to keep up with his long, silent strides, Levet tugged at the hem of his jacket.

"Umm...Roke?"

"Not now, gargoyle," Roke never paused as he made his way toward the back of the cottage. "I've spent the past three weeks being led around like a damned hound on the leash. I intend to savor the moment."

"While you're savoring, I hope that you will recall Sally must have a good reason for—"

"Her reason is to drive me nuts," Roke interrupted, pausing at the side of shed. "I promised her that we would go in search of her father. Together."

"*Oui*. But when?"

Roke clenched his teeth. "In case you've forgotten, she nearly died when the—"

"Vampire-god."

Roke grimaced. The creature that they'd so recently battled might have claimed to be the first vampire, but that didn't make him a god. The bastard had nearly killed Sally in an attempt to break the magic that held him captive.

"When the ancient spirit attacked her," he snapped. "She should be grateful that I was willing to wait for her to regain her strength."

Levet cleared his throat. "And that is the only reason you tried to keep her imprisoned?"

"She wasn't imprisoned," he denied, refusing to recall his panic when Sally had lain unconscious for hours.

Or his fierce reluctance to allow Sally to leave Styx's lair.

"*Non*?" Levet clicked his tongue, seemingly oblivious to how close Roke was to yanking that tongue out of his mouth. "I would have sworn she was locked in the dungeons."

"Not after Gaius was destroyed."

"You mean after she saved the world from the vampire-god?" the gargoyle taunted. "Generous of you."

Oh yeah. The tongue was going to have to go.

"Don't push me, gargoyle," he muttered, allowing his senses to spread outward.

He would deal with the aggravating gargoyle later.

Testing the air, he caught the scent of salty foam as waves crashed against the rocks below, the acrid tang of smoke from the chimney and a distant perfume of a water sprite playing among the whales.

But overriding it all was that tantalizing aroma of warm peaches.

A potent aphrodisiac that once again compelled him forward.

Levet grabbed his back pocket. "Where are you going?"

Roke didn't miss a step as he swatted the pest away. "To get my mate."

"I do not believe that is a good idea."

"Thankfully I don't give a shit what you think."

"*Très bien*," the gargoyle sniffed. "You are the bossy-pants."

"Boss. I'm the boss," Roke muttered, heading directly for the back door.

He'd officially run out of patience twenty one days and several thousand miles ago.

Which would explain why he didn't even consider the fact Sally might be prepared for his arrival.

Less than a foot from the back steps he was brought to a painful halt as an invisible net of magic wrapped around him, the bands of air so tight they would have sliced straight through him if he'd been human.

"What the hell?"

Levet waddled forward, his wings twitching as he studied Roke with open curiosity.

"A magical snare. I've never seen one so strong."

Roke flashed his fangs, futilely struggling to escape.

Damn, but he hated magic.

"Why didn't you warn me?" he snarled.

"I did," the gargoyle huffed in outrage. "You said you were the boss."

Okay, he hated magic and gargoyles.

"You didn't tell me there was a trap."

"You are chasing a powerful witch. What did you expect?" The damned beast dared to smile. "Besides, it's such a fine spell. It would have been a pity to spoil Sally's fun."

"I swear, gargoyle, when I get out of here—"

"Are all vampires always so bad-tempered, or is it just you?" a light female voice demanded, the scent of peaches drenching the air.

Roke swallowed a groan, a complex mixture of fury, lust, and savage relief surging through him.

None of it showed on his face as he turned to study the tiny female with shoulder-length hair that was a blend of deep red tresses streaked with gold. She had pale, almost fragile features with velvet brown eyes and full lips that begged to be kissed.

"Hello, my love," he said in a low, husky voice. "Did you miss me?"

Made in the USA
Lexington, KY
04 July 2014